PRAISE  S

'Concise, beautifully crafted, exquisitely realised pieces . . . Davies' stories feel like those told around camp fires and hearths, on shipboard, in sheepherders' huts and around kitchen tables. They seem familiar while at the same time wholly fresh and original . . . even as we broadly think we know where these stories are going, we can't stop reading for the beauty and the confidence of the prose. Like Chekhov's great stories Davies' stories are deceptively simple. They reward re-reading not by resolving the core mystery, but by revealing layers of meaning and complexity.'
—LADETTE RANDOLPH, editor-in-chief of *Ploughshares*

'A truly original and striking collection. . . . Here is a remarkable voice.'—the 2015 Frank O'Connor Short Story Award judges

'Confirms beyond doubt her position among the finest British exponents of a particularly challenging form.' —*Irish Examiner*

'Extraordinary . . . heart-stopping . . . Like all good stories, these tales expand and reverberate beyond the page, pulsating with life. Davies' voice – witty, offbeat, crackling with intelligence – is entirely her own. No doubt this publication will cement her reputation as one of the finest short story writers in the UK.'
— *New Welsh Review*

'Every story in this stunning collection is a gem and completely unlike what follows or precedes it. Davies' diversity shows no bounds as she takes us from jails in the Wild West to a meeting with Queen Victoria, from Australian isolated farms to snowy Siberia where each time we meet fantastic characters with unlikely and unexpected tales to tell. I loved every single one.'
—SIMON SAVIDGE, 2015 Jerwood Fiction Uncovered Prize judge

'Outstanding . . . perfectly distilled, intense . . . exquisite.'
—*The Yorkshire Post*

'Beautiful, transgressive tales of people colliding with the world.'
—IAN MCMILLAN

'Delicate, magical.'—*Daily Express*

'Extraordinarily powerful.' —V.S. Pritchett Prize Judges: JANE GARDAM, PENELOPE LIVELY and JACOB ROSS

'Darkly funny and unsettling.'—BOYD TONKIN, *The Independent* on *Some New Ambush*

'As if Mark Twain and Annie Proulx had sat down at a desk together. But an original voice too. I shall be looking out for more.'—PIERS PLOWRIGHT

'A writer willing to tackle the hardest of all fictional forms—the short story. This is a region in which so many fail . . . she can do what it is essential to do in this form, create a micro-world, which has reverberations beyond its size and scope, which is metaphysical.'—SARAH HALL

'A true original. Her magical yet weirdly believable stories transport you in a breath into other lives and worlds, without a word wasted.'—MAGGIE GEE

'These stories are so unexpected and compelling it's difficult to find one single word to praise them. Carys Davies deserves every accolade she has received.' —ELIZABETH HARROWER

The Redemption of Galen Pike

THE REDEMPTION
OF GALEN PIKE

Carys Davies

BIBLIOASIS
WINDSOR, ONTARIO

FIRST EDITION
Davies, Carys, author
    The redemption of Galen Pike / Carys Davies.

Originally published : London : Salt, 2014.
Short stories.
Issued in print and electronic formats.
ISBN 978-1-77196-139-4 (softcover).--ISBN 978-1-77196-140-0 (ebook)

    I. Title.

PR6104.A843R43 2017   823'.92   C2016-907609-1
                                                  C2016-907610-5

Readied for the press by Dan Wells
Typeset by Chris Andrechek
Cover Design by Zoe Norvell

Contents

for Michael

THE QUIET

SHE DIDN'T HEAR him arrive.

The wind was up and the rain was thundering down on the tin roof like a shower of stones and in the midst of all the noise she didn't hear the rattle of his old buggy approaching. She didn't hear the scrape of his iron-rimmed wheels on the track, the soft thump of his feet in the wet dust. She didn't know he was there until she looked up from her bucket of soapy water and saw his face at her window, his pale green eyes with their tiny black pin-prick pupils blinking at her through the glass.

His name was Henry Fowler and she hated it when he came.

She hated him sitting there for hours on end talking to Tom about hens and beets and pigs, filling his smelly pipe with minute pinches of tobacco from a pouch in his cracked sheepskin waistcoat, tamping down the flakes with his little thumb, lighting and re-lighting the bowl and sucking at the stem, slurping his tea and

1

sitting there on the edge of his chair like a small obser-
vant bird, and all the time stealing glances at her and
looking at her with his sharp eyes as if he could see right
through her. It filled her with a kind of shame. She felt
she'd do almost anything to stop Henry Fowler looking
at her like that, anything to make him leave and clear
off back to his end of the valley. It felt like the worst
thing in the world to her, him looking at her the way
he did.

He was looking at her now on the other side of the
glass, blinking at her through the falling rain. She wished
she didn't have to invite him in. She wished she could send
him away without asking him in and offering him a cup of
something, but he was their neighbour and he had come
six miles across the valley in his bone-shaking old buggy
and the water had begun to pool around the brim of his
old felt hat and drip onto the shoulders of his crumpled
shirt. It was bouncing back up off the ground and splashing against his boots and his baggy serge trousers. She
would have to offer him a chair by the stove for half an
hour, refreshment. A cup of tea at least. She wiped her
soapy hands on her skirt and went to the door and opened
it and called to him.

'You'd better come in Mr. Fowler. Out of the rain.'

Her name was Susan Boyce and she was twenty-six years
old. It was eight months now since she and Thomas had
sailed out of Liverpool on their wedding day aboard the
Hurricane in search of a new life. It had excited them both,
the idea of starting from nothing. They'd liked the razed,

empty look of everything on the map, the vast unpunctu-
ated distances, and at the beginning of it all she hadn't
minded that the only company was the sound of the wind
and the rain and the crackle of the dry grass in the sunshine. At the beginning of it all, she hadn't minded the
quiet.

She hadn't minded that when they'd arrived in the
town they'd found nothing more than a single dusty
street. No railway station and no church, only an empty
hotel and a draper, a dry goods store that doubled as
a doctor's surgery, a smithy and a pen for market day.
She hadn't minded that when they'd ridden out twelve
miles into the parched country beyond the town they'd
found rocks and gum trees and small coarse bushes and
the biggest sky she'd ever seen and in the middle of it
all their own patch of ground and low, fallen-down
house. She hadn't minded that there weren't other
farms nearby, other wives. She hadn't minded that there
was no one but Henry Fowler, who lived six miles off
and had no wife. No, she hadn't minded any of it and
wouldn't now, she was sure, if things with Tom were
not as they were.

Now she wished there was another wife somewhere
not too far away. Someone she might by this time have
come to consider as a friend; someone she might be able
to bring herself to tell. But there was no such person.
There was her married sister in Poole who she could
write to, but what good would that do, when it might
be a year before a reply came? A year was an eternity;
she didn't think she could last a year, and even then, she

wasn't really sure she could get the thing down on paper in the first place.

Once, a month ago, when she and Tom had gone into town and he was off buying nails, she'd got as far as the black varnished door of the doctor's consulting room in the dry goods store. She'd stood there outside it, gripping her purse, listening to the low murmur of a woman's voice on the other side of the door and she'd tried to imagine her own voice in there in its place and she couldn't. She just couldn't. It was an impossible thing for her to do. What if the doctor said he had to speak to Thomas? What then?

If there'd been a church in town, she might have gone to the priest. A priest, she thought, might be an easy person to tell; but even there, she wasn't sure what a priest would say on such a matter. What if he just told her to go back home and pray? Would she be able to tell him that she'd tried that already? That every night for more than half a year she'd lain in bed and prayed till she was blue in the face and it hadn't worked? Anyway it was a waste of time to think about a priest because there wasn't a church for a hundred miles. It was a godless place they'd come to. Godless and friendless and only Henry Fowler's wizened walnut face at her window at nine o'clock in the morning, poking his nose into her private business.

Well she would not sink under it. No she wouldn't. She'd experienced other setbacks in her life, other disappointments and shocks of one sort or another. It would be the same with this one, she would endure it like anything else, and wasn't it true anyway, that in time all things passed? This would too. There was a remedy, in the end, for everything. She just had to find it.

When she and Fowler were inside she told him that Tom had gone into town for salt and oil and needles and wouldn't be back till nightfall. Fowler nodded and asked if he might tip the water from his hat into her bucket of soapy water.

'Of course,' she said—cold, prim, barely polite.

She invited him to sit, and said she would boil the water for some tea.

At the stove she busied herself with the kettle, wondering what he wanted, why he'd come. She wondered if he was going to sit there and look at her in that way of his that made her want to get up and go somewhere away from him, into a different room, behind a door or a wall or a screen, so he couldn't do it. Somehow it made everything worse, being looked at, especially by someone like Henry Fowler. She'd rarely seen any one who looked as seedy as he did. She wondered if he'd been a convict.

He'd visited them three times before now, once not long after they'd arrived and then again a few months after that, and then a third time just last week. Each time he'd come wearing the same grimy outfit, the same crumpled shirt and ancient sheepskin waistcoat, the same greasy serge pants, the same bit of cotton rag about his thin neck. The only thing she noticed that was different about him today was that he seemed to have brought nothing with him; whenever he'd come to visit them before, he'd always brought some kind of neighbourly gift. The first time it had been a quarter pound of his own butter, the second time a jar of pumpkin seeds. Last time, a loaf. This time his small weather-beaten hands were empty; today Henry Fowler seemed to have brought nothing but himself.

He was forty-five years old—a small, scrawny-looking man with bow legs and rough brown hands no bigger than a woman's.

At sunrise he'd stood with one of those hands resting on the wooden rail of his rickety veranda at the far end of the valley, watching his new neighbour's black horse and dray moving slowly along the road in the direction of the town, wondering if the handsome husband was travelling by himself—if the young wife would be alone there today.

It was six months now since he'd watched them come in on the same road with a pile of furniture tied onto the dray. Since then he'd seen her three times. Three times he'd gone over there with a neighbourly gift. Three times he'd walked about outside with the husband, admiring the progress they'd made. The beets and peas and beans, the potatoes and the fat new pigs. The two hundred chickens, the cow. Three times he'd sat with the two of them inside the house drinking tea and for weeks now he'd been spending the evenings sitting on his veranda and looking out across the grassy desert towards their place.

Susan. That was her name. Susan Boyce. For weeks he'd been thinking about her and practically nothing else. Her stiff, cold, proud-looking face, the closed-off, haughty way she had of speaking to him, the way she couldn't stand him looking at her.

When he could no longer see the dray on the horizon, when it had disappeared completely from view, he went inside for a while and then he laced up his boots and put on his hat and climbed up onto the seat of his high sloping buggy and set off along the track down the valley to her house.

He sat now, at her table, tamping the tobacco into the bowl of his pipe with his little thumb, watching her at the stove.

It's true that Henry Fowler still had the look of a convict about him. He had the look of an old sailor too, and of a fairground monkey someone had dressed up in a pair of pants and a waistcoat and an old felt hat. He was small and sun-wizened and ugly and as he sat now, listening to the wind and the rain and the snuffling of Thomas Boyce's pigs and the crackle of the fire in the stove and the simmering of the water in the kettle on top of it, he was sure he could also hear the beating of his own heart.

The fact is, Fowler was even more nervous now that he was here than he'd expected to be.

His sheepskin waistcoat creaked; he didn't know where to begin. He'd rehearsed everything before he came, had stood for an hour or more before the mirror looking at his own half-naked body, and it had all gone smoothly enough. The words had come without too much difficulty. Now, looking at the other man's wife standing at the stove with her slender back turned towards him, they escaped him.

He took a few quick puffs on his pipe and decided the best thing to do would be to undress.

He took off his waistcoat and placed it over the back of the chair, unknotted the grimy square of cotton he wore folded around his throat and laid that on top of the waistcoat. He undid the buttons on his crumpled linen shirt until the whole thing was hanging down from the canvas belt that held up his trousers, and at that moment Susan Boyce turned. She turned and screamed and dropped the teapot, and covered her mouth with her hand.

Henry Fowler's narrow pigeon chest was lumpy and shrivelled like the map of some strange unknown country. It had a kind of raised border all around it that was ropy and pink; inside it the skin had a cooked, roasted look to it—it was blackened and leathery and hard, like a mummy's, or a creature that has lain for a thousand years in a forgotten bog.

He turned. Three dark triangles the colour of ripe Victoria plums decorated his shoulders; below them and covering most of the rest of his back was another dark shape, also plum-coloured—the puckered print of something large and round.

Low on his hip, just above the canvas belt that held up his trousers, there was a firework splatter of a dozen deep, wrinkled divots.

'My wife,' said Henry Fowler, the words finally coming to his rescue, 'was bigger than me.'

Looking down and behind at his own ruined body he explained how he'd got his blackened chest (a jug of boiling water from the copper), the three dark triangles on his back (her smoothing iron), the big round brand beneath them (the frying pan), the divots (the red-hot poker), and then with his voice dropping very low he told Susan Boyce that there was something else too, below his canvas belt, but he would not show her that. No. If she wanted to guess the worst thing a bad-tempered wife might do with a pair of sharp-bladed dress-making shears, then she would have it.

Susan Boyce said nothing, only looked.

'She is under the beets,' said Fowler quietly—one night when she was sleeping he'd stabbed her through the heart with the sharp stubby blade of a paring knife and carried her outside and buried her with all her things: her skirts and her clogs and the pins from her hair, her frying pan and the jug from the old copper, her iron and the poker and the cutting-out shears and everything else she'd ever owned or touched that reminded him of her and might make him think she was coming for him again—anything that might make him think he could hear the clatter of her furious clogs charging towards him across the hard clay floor.

In town, he said, he'd put it about that she'd run off and left him.

Susan Boyce looked at him.

Her face was still, without expression, and Henry Fowler thought to himself, *I have made a mistake. I am wrong about it all.*

He had been so sure before but now that he was standing in front of her with his waistcoat over the back of the chair and his neck-cloth lying on the seat and his shirtsleeves hanging down like a skipping rope between his knees, Henry Fowler said to himself: *I have watched*

*her here in this house, moving about in her shawl and
her plain high-necked gown, passing behind his chair and
pouring his tea, and I have caught the scent of something
that isn't here, and when he returns tonight she will tell
him what I have told her and he will fetch a few of the men
from town and they will come with their shovels and dig
under the beets and they will look at the marks on me and
I will tell them how I got them and they will look at each
other and remind themselves that Henry Fowler is nothing
but a seedy old convict with a bit of land to his name and
they will shake their heads and call me a liar and then they
will hang me.*

He began to scrabble between his bandy legs for the
cuffs of his shirt, telling himself that as soon as he was
dressed he would climb up into his old buggy and head
off back up the valley and once he was home he would
think about what to do, whether he should sit there on his
veranda and wait until they came for him, or if he should
leave tonight and go somewhere they wouldn't be able
to find him, or if he should come back in the morning
and talk to Boyce and explain things to him in his own
words so he would understand. He bent to the chair where
he'd laid his clothes and picked up his neck-cloth, looped
it behind his dipped head and pushed his arms into the
sleeves of his dangling shirt, and he would have left then,
probably without saying another word, probably just
reaching out for his hat and heading for the door, but by
the time he'd raised himself again and looked up into the
room to where Susan Boyce was standing, she had begun
to unhook her bodice.

She was loosening her skirt and pulling her chemise over her head and undoing the tapes of her petticoats and then she was letting the whole lot slide to the floor around her feet on top of the broken remains of the teapot and its lake of cooling water until she was standing before him in nothing but her woollen vest and her cotton drawers, and then she was taking those off too. She did it quickly, hurriedly, as if she thought she might never again get the chance to show him, as if she thought, even now, he might not be on her side.

She looked smaller, without her clothes, different in every possible way, turning in front of him, displaying the split, puffy flesh of her thighs and buttocks, the mottled green, black and yellow of her belly, the long, weeping purplish thing that started under the hair at her neck and ran down the back of her like a half-made ditch. She came towards him, stepping through the puddle of tea and over the piled-up heap of her things. She took his small brown hand and lifted it to her cheek and closed her eyes like someone who hadn't known till now how tired they were, and then she asked him, would he help her, please, to dig the hole.

ON COMMERCIAL HILL

HE MET HER, my English grandmother, on a chilly summer afternoon on the beach at Southerndown. She was sitting on a rock, on top of her coat, smoking a cigarette and he—I heard this from someone, from Daddy or Mair—was enchanted. He asked her if he could sit down next to her and, no doubt because he was such a big and handsome man, she said yes, and he lit a cigarette of his own and she told him her name, which was Agnes, and he told her his, which was Will.

That day the two of them walked along the road from Southerndown to Ogmore, and from Ogmore over the dunes at Merthyr Mawr to Ewenny, where they watched a pot being fired with a blue treacle glaze, and before she left him to go back to the hotel where she worked, she let him hold her hand.

He came back the next week, and the week after that, and every day that they didn't see each other they wrote to each other, and at the end of four weeks he brought her home for the first time, up on the train to the valleys, and

13

it was there that she discovered something about him that he hadn't told her. Perhaps she overheard it somewhere, or maybe someone made a point of telling her, thinking it was something she ought to know. Anyway, when she asked him about it, he waved his hand and told her it was nothing. It was a daft embarrassing thing that had happened a long time ago, a story about him some people still liked to tell, but it wasn't important and it didn't mean anything any more—the whole thing was a remnant of his youth, something from so long ago he could hardly believe he'd had anything to do with it. Most people had forgotten it and so had he and if anyone ever mentioned it again she should take no notice because he never did any more, and when she said, 'Really?' he said, 'Yes, really.'

Three months after that they were married.

He was thirty-five years old, quite a bit older than she was, and his full name was William Illtyd Parry.

William and Agnes Parry.

They moved into a house on Victoria Street, next to the Co-op, and had three children: the two boys, quickly, first my father Emyr, then my Uncle Tudor, then my Aunty Mair, three years later. I still have a photograph of Will with Mair—at Southerndown again. They are both eating ice-cream. She is wearing a pink ruched bathing suit with a frill around her bottom and he has rolled up his trousers to just below the knee and he is actually wearing a knotted handkerchief on his head. I never knew people really did that till I saw that picture of him. He is holding her hand. He looks happy. He does not look like someone who wants for anything. 'It is enough for me,' he seems to be saying with his sunburned face and his big smile, 'to be standing here on the beach at Southerndown in the sunshine with my baby daughter eating ice cream.'

He worked at the marshalling yard, and at some point he bought the four-room house on Commercial Hill, the one I visited as a child when Agnes was still living there, and people have told me that when he talked about his life at that time he spoke of good suppers and sweet bathed babies and the peace and quiet of the evening. It gave him joy, he used to say, to walk down the high pavements of the sloping streets and feel the mountain in his back and the closeness of the houses in their long staggered rows, the lighted windows of the shops. He never understood why anyone wouldn't want to live their whole life there. He could not think of a better place on earth.

And then the day came when he was promoted at the marshalling yard and he was sent off in the evening to the Red Cow for an hour because Agnes and the children were getting a party ready for him—sandwiches and paper decorations and a cake with candles on it because even though it wasn't his birthday the children begged for candles and Agnes laughed and said, Oh all right then, we can have candles. It was supposed to be a surprise but he knew what they were up to. Mair had spent most of the day behind the settee with a bottle of glue and a pair of scissors and a packet of crêpe paper. All afternoon he'd heard the sound of her trying to be quiet. The boys had shut themselves in the back with Agnes and for hours there'd been a clatter of pans and spoons and jolly shrieks and shouts.

And now he was sitting by himself at one of the brown varnished tables in the lounge bar of the Red Cow when his friends came in, Tom Bara and Cy Fish and Jack Midnight and Will America, all of them looking shifty and serious, and when he said to Tom Bara, 'What is it then, Tom?' Tom looked sideways at the others and then at his feet and said, 'She is back.'

I have often pictured him, nineteen years old, standing there that day in the chapel: dark wavy hair greased neatly in place, neck scrubbed and pink from the bath, starched white collar; waiting. Standing there like an idiot, red-faced and sweating for an hour and a half; everyone whispering and coughing and shuffling their feet and turning their heads to see if she'd arrived yet; some people looking at each other and nodding to indicate that they'd seen it coming, a girl like that. The minister eventually touching his arm and saying, Come on then Will boy, perhaps it's time to call it a day.

'Where is she?' he said now to Tom Bara. Tom shook his head and looked at his feet and then over at the door that divided the lounge bar of the Red Cow from the passage outside.

'Tell her to bugger off, Will,' said Tom. 'Tell her she has come too late.'

At the house Agnes said to Tudor, 'Go fetch your father, we are ready.'

But Tudor was fussing with the cake, and so was Emyr, both of them trying to fit the last of the candles into its metal flower.

'You then,' she called out from the back to Mair, still busy in the front room with her decorations. So it was Mair who ran off up the hill to the Red Cow to call him home; Mair who ran up the hill to the opaque glass door between the outside passage and the lounge bar and found a stranger in a brown hat at the threshold; her father rising slowly from his chair, all his silent friends behind him.

Mair remembers standing there, bits of crêpe paper stuck to her cardigan and her small gluey hands. She remembers that he looked at her and closed his eyes; that a breeze blew in from the passageway, lifting a few strands of his hair, which then settled in a slightly different place, lightly across his forehead. And what she also remembers—Mair who is old now, Mair whose grasp of the here-and-now is getting frailer by the day but whose memory of the past is clear and sharp and fierce and abiding—what Mair remembers is him stepping forward in the stone-still room towards the door, opening wide his arms to her and saying, 'My lovely girl.'

JUBILEE

Standing now at her shoulder, no longer caring much about his future, Arthur Pritt began to speak.

In a quiet voice he apologised for the tediousness of the day, for the marching bands and the pipers, for the choirs and the speeches and the dreadful cacophony of the morris dancers on the cobbles; for the boring gifts. In a whisper he told her he wished they'd been able to conjure something new for her, something splendid and fascinating and unthought of instead of the dull nonsense she must have seen a thousand times before in a thousand other places.

At ten o'clock he had been at the station with the rest of the town to greet her and had known not to expect a happy smiling face. He'd known to expect something miserable and grim-looking, and with her short neck and her pouchy eyes and her sad downturned mouth she'd reminded him, emerging slowly from her compartment, of a hundred-year-old tortoise he and Alice had once seen at the bottom of a dusty pit at the zoo in Calcutta.

He'd wondered if it was true what people said, that she had her husband's clothes laid out for him every morning, his stockings and his shoes, his diamond star, his sash and garter, as if she could not let go of the hope that he would come back to her one day from the dead.

Arthur had never laid out any of Alice's clothes.

He had some of her things that he'd brought back in his trunk from India, a dress and a cotton wrapper that smelled of soap and dust and heat and happiness. He looked at them often, hanging in the armoire in his room, and most days he lifted a sleeve or a hem and held it for a few moments between his fingers. It had never occurred to him though, to lay out any of her things, in spite of his dream that she would come strolling in one day wanting to put them on.

Ahead, in the square, the pipers in their furry head-gear were still at it; he could hear the dismal grating moan of their instruments. The town had been informed that Her Majesty was very fond of a bagpipe but looking at her now, at her grey stony profile, he found that hard to believe. There was the same look on her face as there had been all day—the same look as when she'd sat enduring the shrill repeated notes of the Manchester Flute Band; as when she'd had to put up with the morris men cantering back and forth across the cobbles like escaped lunatics in their noisy wooden shoes, shaking their foolish ribbons and their bells; it was the same look she'd worn through all the shouts and cheers and hoofbeats and the pealing of the church bells; it was a look that seemed to be asking, *When for pity's sake is this all going to end?*

How small she looked on the town's makeshift throne!

How bored and miserable and alone, how remote and marooned and cut off from the world.

All day he'd found himself wishing they'd thought of something in every way more exciting and unusual. Fireworks perhaps. Acrobats, magicians. Anything that would enliven her sad doughy face and bring a sparkle of interest to her half-closed eyes and help her forget, just for a moment, that after all these years she was still bereft.

And then the moment had arrived for the presentation of the gifts—Mr. Boucher's morocco-bound *History of the Town*, Mr. Binns's map of Lancashire, Mrs. Maudesely's commemorative cake—the moment when he, alderman Arthur Pritt, was to stand at the old Queen's shoulder and murmur a few words of introduction and explanation as each new offering was brought up onto the platform.

For a while he had held Boucher's *History of the Town* and quietly turned its gilt-edged pages, hunting for items that might kindle her interest or otherwise lift her leaden spirits. Obediently he had highlighted the illustrations of the linoleum factory, the wallpaper works, the brewery, the old bridge and the new bridge, the Priory and the lumpy piece of ground below the castle where the Roman Baths had once been. The Queen had continued, though, to sit like a stone, a poor unhappy tortoise, and as Binns's map was lifted up onto the crimson-covered platform and propped up before her between two rows of greenhouse plants in their earthenware pots, Arthur had decided he could no longer go on, and glancing quickly at her son the Prince who stood next to his mother on her other side, he began, in a soft whisper close to her ear, to apologise.

His name was Arthur Pritt, he said, and he was sorry for the day.

He was sorry they had not thought of something beautiful and exciting. Fireworks perhaps or acrobats. A magician. He said he wished that in the many, many meetings he'd attended with the other aldermen and the Town Clerk and the Treasurer and the Mayor, and in all the letters that had been exchanged between the Corporation and her Secretary of State on the question of how things should be organised, they had not thought of arranging things a little differently for once.

The Queen's face didn't move. Her mouth seemed locked by its downturned corners into the deepest and most immovable frown.

Binns was kneeling now on the carpet, indicating with a malacca baton the course of the river through the town. On the far left-hand side of the platform, Arthur could see Mrs. Maudesely's vast three-tiered cake on its trolley, ready to make its approach. The Queen had shifted her head slightly and was looking at it, at its profusion of thistles and shamrocks and roses, its expanse of hard white icing like plaster of Paris, and at the lonely little sugar statue of herself balanced on the topmost layer. She looked away, as if the cake had depressed her even more than the bagpipes and the morris dancers. It seemed to produce a lowering effect on her spirits, to have to see herself up there on the cake looking so tiny and isolated and aloof. She rested her chin on her hand, her eyelids drooped. Arthur wondered if she'd heard what he'd said about him being sorry for it all; perhaps she was about to turn to someone from her household and order them to remove him immediately from the platform. Instead she turned a little towards him and said, 'Tell me a story, Mr. Pritt.'

Her son the Prince gave Arthur a sharp look and Arthur hesitated.

'Please, Mr. Pritt. A story.'

So Arthur told the Queen a story, and either because he wasn't an imaginative person, or because the Queen's grief had made him dwell more deeply than ever on his own, or because the time had come when he wanted to tell someone what had happened, he told her a true one, about his wife.

'It was when we were in India,' he told the Queen, 'in Calcutta.'

For the first time all day, a flicker of interest seemed to pass, like a gentle wind, across the Queen's melancholy face. She waved the crouching map-maker away with the point of her fan.

'I left the house as usual one morning,' said Arthur, 'and walked through the city down to the water where the company offices were. When I'd been there an hour, I discovered I'd left some papers behind and went home to fetch them.'

By now Mrs. Maudesely and her helpers had wheeled the gigantic cake into the middle of the platform; the Prince of Wales was leaning down a little towards his mother as if he might be about to ask her to pay attention, but the Queen's hooded eyes were on the balding alderman at her shoulder and without looking at the Prince she flicked her black glove in his direction, a smart reminder that she was the Queen and she would do what she liked.

Arthur explained how he'd expected, on entering the house, to hear the sound of the piano. It was eleven o'clock and at eleven o'clock his wife's piano teacher arrived and stayed till noon, when Arthur came home for lunch and a nap. But the house was quiet, there was no steady beating of fans, the only sound the movement of a broom across the tiles somewhere towards the back of the house or out in the garden. 'Alice?' he called but there was no reply, only the silence of the fans and the distant scraping of the broom. He took off his hat and moved on through the house into the large parlour where his wife's piano stood. 'The lid was open, her music was on the stand. The only thing missing was Alice.'

The Queen nodded. 'Continue, Mr. Pritt.'

Arthur swallowed, his throat felt tight. His robes were hot and heavy. He paused, as if suddenly aware of the strangeness of his situation, but like Macbeth he seemed to have gone on too far now to retreat.

He'd looked into the morning room, he said, where Alice did her reading and planned her menus and wrote her letters and took her sewing but she wasn't there either.

The Queen seemed to be holding her breath, as if she knew now what was coming. Arthur paused, as he always did when he replayed everything in his own mind, picturing himself in his pale linen suit, a frightened sweating figure who seemed to understand by now that his life was coming to some sort of end.

At their bedroom door, he'd stopped. Beyond it he could hear the soft sounds of his wife's pleasure and when he'd bent down and looked in through the keyhole he'd seen her with her head thrown back, a look on her face he'd never seen before; a tangle of flushed white limbs; Miss Gordon, the piano teacher.

One fat hand had flown to the Queen's throat; her pouchy eyes were wide with wonder, as if Arthur had just pulled back a heavy curtain and revealed to her a unicorn, or a talking mirror, or proof of some other astonishing legend.

'Good heavens, Mr. Pritt,' she whispered.

Her blue eyes were fixed on Arthur's face, and for a moment Arthur wondered if she was going to try to console him or comfort him in some way. He was going to carry on, and tell her how Alice had told him afterwards that she wanted to spend the rest of her life with Miss Gordon—Elizabeth, as she now called her—instead of with him, and that he'd been mourning her loss ever since; he was going to tell the Queen that he no longer cared very much about his future, that he missed Alice every minute of every day, and that even this morning, even though he knew she was thousands of miles away in Calcutta still, he'd looked for her face in the crowd.

But the old Queen didn't seem to be interested in what had happened afterwards; she didn't seem to want to hear Arthur talk about his feelings. She seemed lost in a dream of her own; she was looking around at the crimson-draped platform and the walls of the buildings swathed in their yards and yards of flags and patriotic bunting, at the streamers and the barriers, the row upon row of greenhouse plants in their earthenware pots, at the crowds in their Sunday best, waving their white handkerchiefs, at the

Corporation men like Arthur in their embroidered robes, at the people of her own household, at the Secretary of State, at her son the Prince of Wales.

Her mouth drooped and she shook her head.

'Nobody tells me anything, Mr. Pritt,' she murmured softly, and after that it was almost time for her to go, for her train to depart.

At the station Arthur stood with the Town Clerk and the Treasurer and the Mayor and the eleven other aldermen and watched the royal gifts being stowed away: Binns's map, Boucher's illustrated *History* in its purple morocco binding, the enormous cake. He watched and he waved, and when she was gone he threaded his way through the dispersing crowds along the narrow streets of the town and in through the front door of his own empty house.

THE TRAVELLERS

THE LAST TIME it happened, I packed my bags and left. I got on a train at Birmingham New Street and then on another and another and another and I didn't get off until I reached Siberia.

I liked Siberia.

I liked the snow, the quiet.

I opened an inn at the edge of a small town, and catered for the passing trade—a good kitchen with hot stew and boiled potatoes, a downstairs room with a fire and high-backed benches where people could warm themselves and eat their dinner. Upstairs there was a dormitory with six plain but sturdy bunks, and for those in search of a little privacy who were prepared to pay me the extra, two more rooms, each with its own carved and painted single bed. I found a local man, Pyotr, to help me with the heavy work, chopping wood for the stove and the fire and lugging it in from the shed, shovelling snow and seeing to people's horses, repairing their sledges, etc.

I prospered; I didn't miss Birmingham, I didn't miss any one from the office, and whenever I found myself thinking about Geoffrey, well, I just busied myself with something that needed doing, like peeling vegetables or polishing the samovar, or shaking out the big floppy mattresses on the beds upstairs.

My new life was calm.

It was uneventful, and even if I wasn't exactly happy I was at least doing okay. Pyotr was proving himself to be hard-working and reliable and I had settled into a routine; I was enjoying the cooking, my Russian was coming along nicely. I'd started learning the balalaika.

And then, one cold winter's night, very late, when I had washed down the tables and wiped the greasy remains of the meat from the wooden board in the kitchen, when everything was quiet—the six guests who'd come earlier were asleep in their bunks in the dormitory upstairs, the young lawyer who was on his way to Vladivostok was tucked up in one of the single beds, an elderly insurance salesman from Irkutsk in the other—I heard the sound of a sledge, drawing softly to a halt outside the front door.

Pyotr swore; he had just finished tying on his hat, ready to go home. 'It's all right, Pyotr,' I said. 'You go. I can do the fire.'

But Pyotr didn't move; he was staring at the door. I felt a blast of cold air in my back, snow spiralled into the warmth on the freezing wind, a shower of icy flakes landed on my neck and when I turned there he was, steam rising like smoke from his tall fur hat and his long frozen coat: a huge black-haired man, dark and wild like a Cossack, with a beard and a broken nose and narrow glaring eyes and a thin furious mouth—the meanest, most murderously bad-tempered looking person I had ever seen in my life. In one gloved hand he carried a large bone-handled knife with a curved blade that dangled almost to the floor; in the other—a piece of brown paper crumpled into a twisted cone, like a small flowerless bouquet, or the losing end of a Christmas cracker. He asked for vodka.

Pyotr and I began to scurry about, Pyotr going out to the shed for wood to build up the dying fire and back out again to see to the man's horse. I heated up what I had left of the stew and poured vodka into a brown jug and worried about how I was going to tell the terrifying Cossack that I was full for the night, that I had no beds left. Perhaps I could go up and ask the young lawyer if he wouldn't mind squeezing into the dormitory if I put a mattress on the floor and gave him back his money in the morning?

Perhaps—

But I got no further with sorting out the bed problem, because just then Pyotr came back into the kitchen and I knew at once that he had some news to tell me. He was a close, silent sort of man, Pyotr, someone who, though he swore quite a lot, actively seemed to dislike having to speak. On this occasion however I could see that there was something urgent and unavoidable he felt obliged to communicate.

He stood for a while, stamping his boots on the mat to get rid of the snow and untying the laces of his hat from around his chin so that the furry earflaps hung loose on either side of his broad head.

'What is it, Pyotr?' I said. 'What's the matter?'

He nodded towards the other room, where the Cossack was, and over to the little window near the front door.

'A woman.'

'A woman?'

Pyotr nodded. 'Outside. On his sledge.'

I looked. I craned my neck to see over the high backs of the benches in the other room. It was true. There was a shape on the sledge, I could see it through the misted window, hunched into a ball against the whipping of the snow, motionless as a pile of rags.

Over by the fire the Cossack had finished his stew and, by the look of it, the jug of vodka too. He was staring into the flames, brooding and cross. He had taken off his long coat and I could see the curved knife, hanging now from a leather loop attached to the coat's belt.

'Is she dead?' I whispered.

Pyotr shrugged.

I tried to get a better view through the window by rising up on my tiptoes. It was a distance of about twenty feet from the threshold of the kitchen, where I was standing with Pyotr, over to the far wall of the front of the inn where the window was—a small, frost-feathered window with eight thick panes of glass just to the left of the solid front door. To our right, another twenty feet or so away, sat the Cossack, on one of the benches by the fire. Very softly, I took a step out of the kitchen into the room. There. I could see her more easily now. Although it was late, the light was good, the moon shone and the snow was bright, and as I looked, as I craned my neck again to see over the lintel of the window, I thought I saw the heap of rags move.

'Pyotr,' I whispered and nodded towards the window.

This time there was no mistake. The bundle shifted and we saw her face, long and pale like an almond and wrapped tightly round in a dark fringed shawl. Just for a moment, she looked towards the inn; then turned away again and sat like before, motionless and staring straight ahead at some distant point in the snow.

Pyotr was shaking his head and looking uncomfortable. He hated getting involved in the lives of others and had started tying on his hat again.

'Don't go, Pyotr,' I said. 'Please.'

He looked back over at the Cossack, at the knife hanging from his coat. Pyotr shook his head again and took off his hat. I wondered if there was something he wasn't telling me—if he understood these people better than I did and just didn't want to say. You could never quite tell with Pyotr. It was almost impossible to tell what he was thinking at any given moment; what he did or didn't know.

'Do you think he's kidnapped her?' I whispered.

Pyotr shrugged like before. 'Possible.'

I pictured the huge angry Cossack grabbing the woman by the hair while she was walking down the street and forcing her onto his sledge then bringing her here to my little wayside inn against her wishes. I wondered if he was some sort of mercenary—if he had stolen her to order perhaps, and planned to take her in the morning to a secret destination where he would be paid for her delivery. I wondered—

Pyotr nudged me with his elbow. I jumped.

The huge man was on his feet again. Behind him on the low table in front of the fire lay the crumpled piece of brown paper he'd been carrying when he'd first come storming in. He had smoothed it out. I wondered what it was. A letter perhaps? Some sort of contract? A set of instructions? Something, at least, that formed a connection of some sort between him and the woman?

He was standing now with his back to the fire. I could see his face. He had pushed his wild black hair back from his forehead and as we watched him through the open kitchen door, he rubbed his cheeks and forehead vigorously with his big hands, as if he were washing his face— the way people do when they are tired and want to revive themselves before beginning some new and necessary task. He let out a big sigh. Then he put on his coat, walked over to the door, and went back out into the snow.

It was falling more thickly now. The woman, in her shawl, had begun to resemble a big white stone. A black dog had come trotting out from the town and was sniffing around at the base of the sledge.

I opened the front door a crack behind the man. The wind had died away and when he spoke we heard him clearly.

'You will freeze,' he was saying to her in a flat toneless voice. 'In the morning I will come and you will be nothing but a block of ice. A frozen statue.'

I could see now that she was very beautiful, but also that she was as angry as he was. Both of them had exactly the same expression—sullen, furious, unyielding. She hated him and he hated her back. You could feel it, plain as anything, the poison between them—a bitter, resentful mutual loathing that seemed ready at any moment to turn into something much, much nastier.

The Cossack took a step forward, the dry snow squeaked beneath his boot. 'You should come in now,' he said.

The woman raised her chin. 'No.'

'Then you will die.'

His words hung between them in the freezing night; it occurred to me that it was the cold and nothing else that had brought him out to her. It wasn't because he wanted to be the one to make peace between them; everything about him was grudging and reluctant; he was as morose and brimful of dislike as she was; it was only the danger she was in that had made him come out—the dark travelling shawl she had on might have been good enough for the day but it would not see her through the night. He stood there for another few minutes while she remained seated on the sledge, mulishly still as before. At one point he held out his hand to her in a cool, unwilling kind of way but when she didn't take it he let it fall, and in one final furious gesture, he took off his coat and threw it, knife and all, onto the sledge, so it covered her shoulders like a blanket, and then he came marching back into the inn, alone.

Inside, on the low table by the fire, the piece of brown paper lay as before. The man picked it up now, folded it, and put it away inside his shirt. He didn't ask if I had a room, he just wrapped his giant's arms around himself and leaned against the high back of the bench and sat there, glaring into the fire.

Sometimes I wonder if at some half-conscious level, I knew then what had happened between them.

If I did, I wasn't aware of it; when I discovered the truth, it came to me, I swear, as a revelation.

I didn't go to bed. From time to time during the night and early morning I looked out through the window at the woman on the sledge. It was one of the drawbacks of the inn that we had no covered place for the horses and the sledges, only an open shelter with a beaten tin roof which kept out some of the wind but not the cold and not much of the snow. She wasn't wearing the man's coat. It lay behind her like a big dead animal. Still she sat, straight as a pole, though as the hours passed, her body began to shake. Around two o'clock the snow stopped falling; it was too cold now for snow. A crust of ice formed on the leather traces of the sledge and around the woman's shawl and on the tops of her boots.

Twice in the night I went out with Pyotr, once with a fur wrap and once with some stew; she thanked us for both but when I said, would she come in out of the cold and sit by the fire? she shook her head.

'Not if he's in there.'

Towards morning we went out for the last time.

The stone pillars of the town gates were grey against the yellow sky, snow filled the thick clouds but none had come down now for several hours. Something had happened though, to the woman.

She lay now, in the bottom of the sledge. The black dog that had come in the night sat on her feet, as if trying to keep them warm. But she was frozen hard; her hair, when I lifted a piece that had slipped out from her shawl onto her face, snapped between my fingers like a frozen reed. I prised open the crisp folds of her clothing—the fur wrap, her grey woollen shawl—and found her hands. I began to chafe them with snow.

Pyotr watched, frowning. 'Stop,' he said. 'Let Pyotr.'

He was strong, Pyotr. Short and stocky and wide. Even so, he couldn't move her. He put his arms around the lumpy parcel of her body but it seemed to cling with a kind of obdurate force to the sledge. She was frozen and stuck to it. He went inside and came back with a rope, looped it around her and pulled. There was a sharp snap as she broke free from the ice and then he lifted her in his arms and carried her, like a small frost-covered pine tree, into the warm.

The fire was low now, there were just a few embers left glowing in the grate. Mostly it was ash. I raked up what was there and threw on a new log. The Cossack was still sitting up but he was dozing now. Pyotr laid the frozen woman at his feet by the hearth.

Under the fur wrap and her woolly grey shawl she had on one of those pretty, brightly embroidered dresses, like the ones the Sadler's Wells dancers had worn when Geoffrey took me to see *The Rite of Spring* a few years before for my birthday. The most striking thing about her, though, was her face, still furious and indignant, gazing out from beneath a thin carapace of ice, like something trapped in a pond, or behind the clouded glass of an old mirror. The effect was curious and unsettling; it was clear to me now that she was dead.

On the bench beside me the Cossack no longer slept. He was sitting without moving, just staring at the body of the frozen woman at his feet.

Pyotr grunted. He bent to the floor to pick up his rope, which was lying in a sodden coil on the hearth. I didn't know what to say. For something to do I began to gather up the remains of the Cossack's dinner—his bowl and cup, his fork and spoon, the empty vodka jug—and perhaps it would all have ended there if I hadn't noticed then the piece of paper on the floor beneath the bench, the one the man had carried in his fist and later folded and put inside his shirt. It must have fallen out while he slept.

I picked it up, opened it. It was a map. A maze of hand-drawn tracks across the snowy wilderness, an arrow in the right-hand corner, pointing north. I thought of the Cossack's smouldering fury when they arrived, of the woman's suicidal six-hour sulk in the snow and then I understood; everything that was familiar about the two of them seemed at that moment to reveal itself. Even before the Cossack glanced over and saw me holding the map, even before he'd shrugged his massive shoulders and thrown up his hands and gestured towards the window at their sledge parked outside, even before he'd opened his mouth to speak, I knew what he was going to say:

'Always when we drive, my wife and I, we argue.'

I thought of Geoffrey.

I thought of our last horrible scene in the car after his brother's wedding in Salford, after I'd told him to come off the M6 just north of Manchester at junction 26 and go into Wigan; after we'd got lost in Wigan and been stuck in traffic for an hour and three quarters in the centre of town, then trailed slowly on for another hour through Hindley, Atherton and Tyldesley, and ended up arriving at the church when the wedding ceremony was just finishing; I thought of how we'd sat through the reception without speaking a word to each other and then walked silently back to the car, of how Geoffrey had taken the road atlas out of the compartment in the door on my side and said to me in that quiet voice that pretends to be patient and understanding but is in fact a hair's breadth away from being speechless with incandescent fury, 'Why would you do that, Harriet? Why wouldn't you tell me to come off at junction 21a and then take the M62 all the way up to the M602 into Salford? Or junction 20 so I could have taken the M56 and picked up the western ring road until we hit the M602 there and gone in that way? *Jesus Christ, Harriet*, why would you take us in through the centre of Wigan on a Saturday morning?'

I remembered how I'd turned away from him and stared out of my window at the trees and the departing wedding guests and the other cars in the hotel car park and said, quietly, as he had, 'It seemed like the best way to me, Geoffrey.'

I thought of the five hours we'd spent on the Boulevard Périphérique in Paris. I thought of the horrible, fat Michelin book with its hundreds of pages, each one with a small piece of Paris on it so that the road kept running off the edge of one page and on to another but never onto the next page, always onto a different page somewhere else in the book that you could only find by consulting the index at the back and by the time you'd found it, it was too late. I thought of Geoffrey's demented shouting as we went whipping past the Saint-Cloud exit for the fourth time. *Shall I come off here, Harriet? Shall I? Shall I? Tell me what I need to do Harriet, you need to tell me, you need to tell me, you need to tell me NOW. Look! There's the exit. You need to tell me now now now now now oh too late.* I thought of the evening we drove down to London for a seven-thirty performance of *Oklahoma!* at the National Theatre; of how at around eight o'clock, somewhere between Hendon and Cricklewood, Geoffrey stopped the car and pulled over and switched on the overhead map-light and without a word put his hand out for the *A to Z*; how he turned over a few pages and studied them and then handed me back the book and extinguished the light and moved slowly off again into the traffic. I thought of the satellite navigation device Geoffrey had bought, not long after his brother's wedding, and what high hopes I'd had of it, but it too had been shouted at, and then banished, for choosing the wrong way and taking us to places we didn't want to go, and after a short time we'd gone back to doing things the way we'd always done them, and I thought, now, of the hundreds of occasions when things had gone badly for us in the car. I thought of how, somehow, the between-car-journeys bit of our life suddenly became an unimaginably distant thing; I thought of how every single time it happened, my heart shrivelled up into a tiny dry peanut without the tiniest drop of love left inside it for Geoffrey, until the only thing left to do was to show him the back of my head and stare out of the window on my side and cry and silently repeat the chant, *I hate you Geoffrey Parker, I hate you, I hate you, I hate you.*

Next to the fire, the Cossack stared sadly at the body of his dead wife. Pyotr had fetched a mop and was dabbing gently at the wet floorboards around her where the ice from her clothes had begun to thaw.

Upstairs in the dormitory the bunk beds creaked. People were getting up. Soon they would be down, the young lawyer on his way to Vladivostok and the old salesman from Irkutsk and the others, wanting their breakfast. Well, I would make breakfast. I would fill the samovar and give them hot tea and fresh rolls. I would send Pyotr into town for the carpenter and the priest and when he got back I would say to him that I was very sorry but I was going back to Birmingham now. I would tell him that he could keep the inn if he wanted it, I would leave everything for him, the beds and the cooking pots, the crockery, the vodka jugs, the knives and forks, the wood pile in the back, my balalaika, and then I would pack my bags. I would walk out into the snow and climb on the first train that was heading west out of Siberia and I would keep going until I got back to Geoffrey, and once I was there I would do what I should have done years ago, I would have some driving lessons, and when I passed my test, I would drive, and Geoffrey would navigate. And if I failed my driving test, I would take Geoffrey's hands in mine and tell him I loved him. I would make us a good dinner and open a bottle of wine, I would put on the blue Margaret Howell linen blouse he gave me for our twelfth wedding anniversary and the cedar-wood bracelet he gave me for our fifth, and I would talk to him about public transport.

MYTH

IT WASN'T LIKE you think.

When the time came I was brought to the queen's tent and told to lie down on the couch.

The whole place was lit with tapers and it was bright as day. All the other women were there, standing in rows on the carpeted ground—to give me strength, said the queen. She herself bound my wrists and ankles and secured them to the couch. I was given a beaker of cordial to drink and after that I can't tell you how long it seemed before the Chinaman arrived.

When he did I began to shake. My feet bucked against the leather straps and my gorge rose.

'No,' I said. 'I prefer to die,' but the queen shook her head and the little Chinaman asked for water.

He was tiny. A minute person in a soft blue tunic and a bamboo hat who had once set the queen's broken leg. Black cotton shoes on his neat little feet, in his hand a hide bag with a pleated neck holding his instruments.

'I will cover your face and be very quick,' he'd told me

the day before and shown me the ivory comb he would place between my teeth.

He would need dry sponges, he said, and plenty of light; a bucket.

He seemed anxious now.

Anxious and uneasy and reluctant.

I saw him glance at the queen, as if he hoped for some kind of last-minute reprieve, but all she did was nod and point with her muscled finger at his little bag.

He bowed and took out his ink-stone; moistened it. From an invisible pocket in his tunic he produced a cloth and put it over my eyes.

I felt the point of his brush, trembling and wet, describe a circle for his knife to follow and then he made the first cut.

It must be a horrible thing to carve off a piece of a living person who has only the benefit of a beaker of strong wine to steady them.

Five times I counted he went in with his knife, pushing and pulling and sawing and—oh—just when I thought it was over, scraping away at the bone beside my heart to take the last of it.

Half the women fainted, their big broad-shouldered bodies going down like trees and through it all the clatter of their spears and bows falling against each other, arrows dropping like pins from their upturned quivers.

The air stirred and the Chinaman's cloth slipped from my face. I saw the queen sway beside the couch. She looked ill and green and when the diminutive doctor asked her humbly, would she be next? she seemed embarrassed.

She toyed with the tassel of her golden girdle and coughed a little; mumbled something about second thoughts and changing her mind.

Told him, in a quiet voice, that he could go now—that some of her ideas, perhaps, were better than others.

(The suggestion that the Amazons removed one breast— either by cutting or burning, in order to enhance their prowess on the battlefield—is a persistent one; however there is no indication of such a practice in works of art, in which they are always represented with both breasts, though the right one is often shown covered.)

BONNET

It's early when she boards the London train—dark when she leaves the house and still dark when she arrives at the station in Leeds and enters her compartment and nods to her fellow passengers.

What do they see, her fellow passengers?

They see a small, plain, obscure woman in a black travelling outfit, on her head a large funnel-shaped bonnet, also black, with a dark grey lining—a small, plain, obscure-looking woman who has been to London several times before and has no plan when she gets to her lodgings to do anything differently from the last time or the time before that or the time before that.

It's only the next morning when she is walking along Gracechurch Street that she decides to do it—and even then it doesn't feel like a decision, it feels like she is being carried along on a wave of something she cannot help.

For a long time she stands there before going in. She knows that in a great many ways she has led a sheltered life and that there are plenty of things she doesn't know, such as the right places to go for certain things. Even now, when she comes to London, she feels most of the time like a clumsy traveller in a foreign land.

She can see herself in the glass: her black travelling outfit, her big dark bonnet with its grey lining; her reflection very clear in the sparkling window.

How clean the window is!

She herself has been doing a lot of cleaning lately. When she can't write, and these days she cannot seem to write a single line, cleaning feels like a good productive thing to do.

Still not quite knowing what she'll do when she gets inside, she pushes open the door.

He wants to talk to her, he said in his letter, about her next book. The appointment is at four o'clock which means she has two hours.

As soon as she's inside, the bell on the door ringing out its last chimes behind her, she knows why she's come.

The choice is bewildering.

'That one,' she says, pointing, after much deliberation over the possibilities, and takes the money from her purse. A huge amount, it seems, for such a thing. And then she takes off her bonnet, and puts it on the counter and watches it being taken away through the curtain, and sits, and waits till it's ready. She feels naked, without her bonnet; almost asks if there is one she can borrow while she's waiting.

At a quarter to four she leaves the shop, her bonnet back on her head, and makes her way along Gracechurch

Street and from there to Cornhill to attend the meeting that is due to take place at four with her young publisher.

He has written her a letter, her tall, dark-haired, handsome young publisher, but she has not received it.

Not the letter asking if they can meet to talk about her next book.

Another letter, a second letter.

It was early when she left home yesterday and climbed into her compartment, first at Keighley, then at Leeds, and she has not received this second letter, as he had expected she would have, before her visit.

A second letter in which he's told her the news that he has fallen in love with a Miss Elizabeth Blakeway and is engaged to be married.

He is standing behind his desk when she is shown into his office, a collection of papers in his hand.

His pale complexion is flushed from his morning ride in the park, and in the half-second it takes for him to look up from his reading, she takes him in afresh: his rangy, athletic height, his youthful, generous, intelligent, shrewd and sensitive face.

Never, in her whole life, has she been as conscious of her own appearance as she is at this moment—and she is always *always* acutely and painfully conscious of her own appearance when she is with him here in London, here in his office or having dinner with his mother and his sisters, or out in public, at the opera, or at an exhibition or at some terrifying literary party; but she has never, ever, been as conscious as she is now of her own tiny body and large, ill-proportioned head; her crooked mouth and her thin hair, bulked up with its little pad of stuffed brown silk—of her big nose, of her spectacles, of her age, or of how until this moment, she has never appeared before him in anything other than black or grey.

It is pink, the new lining of her bonnet—a lustrous, pearly pink like the interior of a shell, and it is the worst imaginable thing, when he looks up, for him to see it; for him to see this small plain woman, his friend, with this unexpected bonnet on her head.

For a moment he is speechless—all he can do is stand there looking at her and wishing that he could tell her something, the future perhaps—that before she dies in eighteen months' time, at the age of thirty-eight, she will marry and be so happy, eventually, in this brief, late marriage with her quiet clergyman husband, that she will not care if she never writes another word; but he knows nothing of her future—nothing that could come now to her rescue or to his, and all he can do is to move towards her and shake her hand with what he hopes is all his usual warmth and invite her to sit, and for an hour they talk about her books, and the books of other people—they have always got along so well together, their discussions have always been so lively and full of interest—and he says nothing about the bonnet and neither does she but it is the worst imaginable thing for her to sit and feel the bright new silk around her face, like a shout, and see how embarrassed he is, how he can't look at it.

It's late when she boards the night train—dark when she leaves her lodgings and arrives at Euston Square and enters her compartment and nods to her fellow passengers. By six the next morning she is a world away, in Leeds, and by eight in Keighley again where, unable to face the prospect of being collected in the Haworth gig, she begins at once the long walk home, keeping her eyes down to avoid her reflection in shop fronts and the windows of houses. It has been raining though, here in the north. There are puddles everywhere, and she is in all of them: a small, plain, obscure-looking woman in a black travelling outfit, on her head a large funnel-shaped bonnet, also black, with a dark grey lining.

FIRST JOURNEYMAN

(Responsible for fruits, plants and legumes)

WHAT CAN I tell you?

That he was seventeen years old; that in the morning he top-dressed the Melon Pit with a compost of turf, lime rubble, charcoal, wood ash, clay and bone dust. That he rolled the drive and cleaned out the pond, and put a small stake to the Chrysanthemums to prevent the wind from breaking them; that after that he watered the Trees in the Peach Case and dusted the berries with sulphur to keep the mildew down.

That Jenny came out then, asking for something sweet and tasty for Master B who had a summer cold and was keeping to his room with books and a hot water bottle and was after something to tempt his appetite.

That he went off and came back with a leaf of mint and a pound of First Peas, Sutton's Bountiful, in a white dish, and sent them in for Master B, and that all through our dinner he was very quiet and hardly touched his food; that in the afternoon he mowed the tennis court and made up the vases for Thursday's party and tied up the kidney beans and cleaned the glass in the Rose House and shifted a few Gloire de Lorraine out of 3" into 5½" pots. And in the evening, on our way home when we called in at the back door for a cup of water, he asked Jenny if Master B had enjoyed the Peas and Jenny, pushing back her hair and wiping her old hands on her apron, said, What Peas? and he, kicking the toe of his boot against the doorstep and looking down at it, said, The Sutton's Bountiful, from this morning, and Jenny frowned as if she couldn't think what he was on about and then she smacked the heel of her hand against her forehead and said, Oh *them* Peas! Oh no—hadn't we heard? Master B's cold was better now and his American friend Mr. Slade had come and fetched him back off to London again before the Peas was eaten.

Oh, he said.

And I could see them then, the Peas, behind her. A gleam of green on the table, still in the white dish he'd put them in with the sprig of mint on top, like some sort of offering, and all I can tell you is that it must have seemed a big thing to him, what had happened.

All I can say is that it must have seemed to him, somehow, like the end of the world.

PRECIOUS

FROM THE MOMENT I arrived, they loved me.

They loved my funny accent, the way I had ketchup with everything. They loved my black socks and my brown sandals; they loved my flesh-coloured money-belt, my grey wheeled suitcase with its retractable handle. Most of all though, they loved the way I sweated in the heat, the way the hot sun made the pale dome of my head glow like a lightbulb. They loved the sight of it, and when they touched it, it brought a smile to all their faces.

Within a week the mayor had installed me in an apartment on the top floor of his mansion and employed an extra cook and a housekeeper to look after me; queues formed every morning at first light outside the mansion's tall iron gates, and throughout the day the townspeople came to touch my head. It was extraordinary, the pleasure it gave them, the way it made them smile. Little by little they began expressing their appreciation with gifts—homemade bread and custard flans, bottles of wine, sausage, cash; it wasn't long before they began requesting my presence at important events: birthdays and retirement parties and the unveiling of a new fountain in the market square, at baby showers and at weddings. They even wanted me at their funerals to stand by the open coffin of the deceased when they came to say their goodbyes. It cheered them up, they said, to be able to touch my head after kissing the body for the very last time. By the end of the summer there was hardly a single public occasion that took place without me and I—well, I had begun to feel slightly uncomfortable with the situation.

It bothered me that they thought so much of me, and while I tried to remind myself that I had never once claimed to be anyone special, I couldn't help feeling, as the months passed and they took me ever more passionately to their hearts, that I was moving, slowly but surely, towards some kind of frightful unmasking or exposé; that each day was bringing me closer and closer to my own humiliating demise.

I decided I'd better leave, before things got out of hand.

I decided I would slip out of my apartment one night while the cook and the housekeeper and the mayor were all asleep. I would walk out of the town on the road I'd come in on and I would go to a different place—a quiet beach or a little chalet up in the mountains—somewhere I wouldn't attract quite so much attention.

And I would have gone, I really would have. I even got as far as putting a few things in my wheeled suitcase, ready for my departure. But then the people sent me

Precious and once they'd sent me Precious, I just couldn't tear myself away.

Precious was the daughter of the cook and she arrived very early one September morning before the queues had begun to form outside. I knew at once that she had come for some important reason because she was shown up to my apartment not in the clunky old service elevator at the back which her mother the cook and the housekeeper and all the other townspeople were made to use, but in the beautiful hand-operated Schindler elevator at the front with its fitted carpet and gilded paintwork and its twinkling chandelier.

When I opened my apartment door that morning there she was—a small, serious-looking girl with dark hair and a pale face, wearing a floral cotton dress and holding a large black leather bag with a metal clasp, like an old-fashioned doctor's. As soon as she saw me she blushed and bobbed a sort of curtsey and told me that she had come to polish my head.

Everyone, she explained, wanted it to be as bright and soft as possible and they would all be very pleased if I would allow it to be polished first thing every morning. She was very good at polishing, she said, blushing again, and had been specially chosen by the people for the job. She would come every morning and do it before the crowds came, if I was agreeable.

I looked at her.

I looked at her shy serious face, her dark eyes with their grave almost sad expression, at her small neat fingers on the stitched handle of her bag, and as I looked, I forgot the anxiety I'd begun to feel about my strange position in the town; I forgot the certainty I'd felt, just the night before, that it was time for me to get out of there; I forgot the half-packed suitcase lying open on the velvet armchair in the sitting room behind me, waiting for me to pick it up and wheel it out of the door.

'Yes,' I said, smiling. Of course I was agreeable.

Precious's visits became the highlight of my days.

As soon as I opened my eyes in the mornings, I began listening out for the slow whirring progress of the Schindler elevator bringing her up. Hearing her knock at my door—seeing her there when I opened it—watching her set down her big doctor's bag on the carved chest beneath the window and take out her pots of wax and her various creams and cloths—hearing her asking me, in her quiet way, to please take a seat so she could begin—these were the things I lived for. I looked forward to them more than anything else in the world. The rest of my days—the birthday parties, the baby showers, the weddings, the funerals—all of it passed in a dull blur, and I can honestly say that I was never happier in my whole life than when Precious was there, close to me, moving around my chair, turning away from time to time to pick up a different pot or a fresh cloth, asking me to tip my head a little to the left or a little to the right, forward or back.

My only difficulty was that I had no idea what she thought of me. She was always so shy and deferential in my presence—so silent and business-like in the way she went about her work—that it was impossible to tell what was going on inside her head, let alone her heart.

If I ever tried to make eye contact with her while she polished, she blushed and looked away and focused instead on whichever part of my scalp she was busy with at the time. When she was finished she packed her things away in her big bag and bobbed another of her funny little curtseys and left.

At the end of six weeks we had hardly exchanged a single word; I still had no idea what she thought of me, if she had grown even the slightest bit fond of me during our time together. For all I knew, I meant no more to her than any other object she'd been asked to polish; for all I knew I was no more important to her than a brass candlestick or a canteen of silver cutlery.

And then one day, as she was bending over me so that her cheek was quite close to mine, I saw that her eyes were full of tears.

'Precious?' I said softly. 'Is there something the matter?'

At first she shook her head and continued polishing as before, but after a while her tears began to pour down over her face. She let go of her cloth and it fell from her hand onto my lap. She hung her head and chewed her lip, and then she looked up into my eyes as if she had something serious and important to say but lacked the courage to do so.

'Precious?' I repeated gently, but again she shook her head.

'It doesn't matter,' she said, and with that she picked up the cloth from my lap and dropped it into her big open bag and snapped it shut and left.

When the people came that morning I could hardly sit still while they filed past, laying their loaves of bread at my feet, their bottles of wine, their envelopes of cash, patiently queuing for their quick turn with my head. I found myself wriggling beneath the touch of their hands; all I could think about was Precious, and what might have happened to make her cry. I couldn't stop thinking that it must have something to do with me—that in the course of all the silent time we'd spent together she had finally fallen in love with me but was too shy, or too constrained by the relationship between us, to be able to tell me.

I was a fool of course, but I expect you've gathered that already.

I expect, with all your experience of the world, that you can see how things were beginning to shape up; that you have a pretty good idea, by now, of what lay in store for me. But for the moment let me tell you that all I wanted to do then was to find Precious and tell her that I loved her too, and ask her to come with me somewhere else where we could forget about everything that had happened here, somewhere where we could both find some sort of fulfilling work and settle down and live quietly together and be happy.

When the last of the townspeople left my apartment that day, and the housekeeper had loaded the last of their offerings onto her trolley and wheeled it off to the big clanking service elevator at the back and taken it down to the storage rooms in the basement, I went to my dressing room to change: there was a wedding that evening and I had been booked to attend it; the bride, I knew, was a cousin of Precious; Precious would be there among the guests; I would find her and I would speak to her and it would, I felt sure, be the end of one life and the beginning of another.

It seems pointless now to tell you how elated I felt as I strode out that day through the tall gates of the mayor's mansion and threaded my way through the narrow streets of the town. It seems pointless now to tell you anything other than what happened when I got to the wedding.

By the time I arrived the guests were all gathered in the yard of the bride's house—one of those little houses that cling to the side of the hill behind the town, two tiny wrought-iron balconies on the windows of the upper floor filled with bright geraniums; a small courtyard behind with acacia trees.

I took up my position next to the groom beneath a canvas canopy that had been erected in the yard for the ceremony and looked around for Precious. I couldn't see her anywhere. I looked at every face, craned my neck to see if she was hidden somewhere behind another person, or one of the trees. I squinted at the four small dark windows at the rear of the house to see if she was inside somewhere, and my eyes were still searching for her when the bride, dressed in a simple white frock and carrying a bouquet of lavender, appeared with her father at the back door of the house.

For one horrible moment, I thought it was Precious. My stomach lurched. I felt sick.

I blinked and looked again.

No. It wasn't her. Her cousin was rather like her, that was all—small and dark, with the same neat hands and feet; the same shy expression in her downcast eyes. Slowly she began, this cousin, to approach me on her father's arm, and the relief I'd felt on realising that she wasn't Precious turned quickly to impatience and irritation as she placed her small palms on top of my scalp and I watched the inevitable broad smile spread across her face. My head felt waxy and unpleasantly warm. I braced myself for the bridegroom's hand as it too came down, big and sweaty, like a hot heavy flannel, a half-cooked pancake. I told myself to be patient as he also began to smile; I told myself it didn't matter if my skin had begun to crawl the way it had earlier that day when Precious had left and all the townspeople had come. I told myself that it didn't matter if I felt as if I couldn't bear for another second to stand between the two of them with their hands on my head, that it didn't matter if I knew beyond any shadow of a doubt that I didn't want to do this any more, because very soon, it would all be over. I would find Precious and we would leave. I gritted my teeth and looked at the ground, repeating to myself that it would all be finished very soon. I took several deep breaths. One, two, three, and at last managed to achieve a kind of calm, a feeling of patient expectation—a sort of quiet, thrilled excitement at the thought of everything I had to look forward to—and then, quite suddenly and quite without warning, the shouting began.

I felt the sticky palms of the bride and groom stiffen with surprise, and when I raised my eyes there, in the crowded courtyard, was Precious, and she was shouting.

She was standing at the back near the house on what looked like an empty champagne box. In one hand, she held a glass of wine and my first thought was that she seemed rather drunk. She was swaying slightly from side to side, splashing wine on the shoulders of the guests around her. Her speech was slurred, and it was difficult, at first, to make out what she was saying. The crowd too had started to murmur which made it even harder to hear her but after a little while, as they listened more closely to what she was saying, their voices began to die away and I could distinguish her words clearly. She was talking about me. She was talking about my head.

How come, she was shouting, she always felt so miserable when she was touching it?

How was it, that in all the hours she'd spent in the plush apartment of the mayor's mansion, bent over my head, touching it non-stop, it had never once brought a smile to her face?

How was it that in all those weeks she'd been schlepping that huge leather bag up and down in the fancy gold elevator she'd never once gone away any more cheerful than when she'd arrived?

Surely, she shouted, if my head was so marvellous, then she, of all people, would be feeling a bit happier by now?

A silence had fallen over the courtyard. All the guests had turned to look at me; I felt all their eyes upon me.

Precious lowered her voice and I heard her say to them, wasn't I actually just a dull Englishman with no hair? A lonely tourist with tea-cup ears and poppy-out eyes?

Wasn't I actually just a nothing, a nobody, a useless piece of rubbish, a complete and utter waste of all their time?

I swallowed.

I whispered her name.

I stretched out my hand towards her but she didn't move, she just stared at me, and then one of her uncles stepped forward and picked up a rock from the dusty ground of the garden and threw it at her—a swift hard blow that caught her in the throat and sent her flying off her little box like a skittle, or a coconut, and then all the other guests began to close in around her, pushing and jostling and hurling everything they had, handbags and wedding gifts and glasses of wine and bottles of champagne, branches snapped from the acacia trees and poles torn out from under the canvas bridal canopy, more rocks from the dusty ground, and when at last they had finished and dispersed there was almost nothing left of her—a single shoe, a tattered strip of fabric from her cotton dress, some scraps of ragged flesh and splintered bone.

In my dreams I save her.

In my dreams I have seen what's coming and know how to prevent it. In my dreams I am quicker and stronger than they are—I do not stand there in the garden like a frozen lump, shocked and terrified and appalled.

In my dreams I do not have a new girl who comes to polish my head—in my dreams the mayor does not come with her in the early mornings to unlock my door; he does not stay to keep an eye on things when the people arrive with their gifts. He does not drive me himself to whatever functions are on in the afternoon and evening, he does not return with me to lock up my apartment for the night, he does not post his beefy guards beside both elevators, front and back, he does not tell me that I must never think of trying to leave them. He does not remind me that I am dear to them, that they love me and cannot live without me—that outside beyond the tall iron gates of his mansion, armed bands roam the countryside, hunting down anyone who dares to insult the name of The Bald One.

THE TAKING OF BUNNY CLAY

NANCY LIKED THAT there were no fences between the houses, that everything was open.

Maybe when Bunny was older they would need to put something up, so he could play out, but for now she liked it the way it was—the wide, quiet, almost car-less avenue in front that ran down to the harbour and the town.

Sometimes at night, on the hot July evenings in the weeks before Bunny was born, she and Beecham used to walk down to the harbour and sit near the tethered boats, their tinkling masts, look out across the calm silvered water, and it was hard to believe they could be so close to any kind of city; that the moving lights in the distance beneath the canopy of stars belonged to the planes dropping down one after another into the airport, and weren't the last gently cascading points of a ship's flare way out in the middle of the ocean.

Into this unfenced and starlit world Cheryl had come, a recommendation from a neighbour of Nancy's friend Mary-Katherine in New Rochelle.

'Heavy but reliable' was this neighbour's description of Cheryl, which at the time had sounded to Nancy like faint praise, but in the event she'd fallen instantly and gratefully under the spell of the girl's statuesque solidity, the calm and solemn expression that covered her broad mahogany-coloured face.

A European girl had arrived two weeks after Bunny was born but she'd been so volatile and unpredictable in her moods they'd sent her back. After that, Cheryl's slow-moving steadiness, her absolute evenness of temper, had felt like a balm.

Beecham, too, was impressed and reassured by Cheryl's stately bulk, the way she loomed, silent and impassive, at the door every weekday morning without fail at six forty-five. He was even a little fascinated by her appearance. She had the sturdiest, most powerful-looking legs he had ever seen on a woman. Her calf muscles were so large and firm they practically made a right angle above her ankles. Nancy, in her suit and pumps, looked like a twig next to her. On her bare feet, the girl wore a pair of floppy tan plastic sandals that made a sound like a soft broom sweeping sand across their polished oak floors. She radiated a kind of imperturbable peace. She hardly spoke. Very occasionally, when their paths crossed in the early mornings, Beecham Clay wondered what went on in her head, what she made of them. But for the most part, he didn't give the girl a great deal of thought; she was Nancy's to think about; she was there, in their house, for thirteen hours a day and Nancy seemed happy with the arrangement; her return to work, after all the anxiety over the European girl, had been easier than he'd expected.

How did she seem to you then, Beecham, this Cheryl?

Oh, heavy but reliable. That's probably what Beecham Clay would say now about Cheryl Toussaint if you could ask him.

Maybe it was because Cheryl reminded Nancy so much of her mother's maid, Iceline, that she took so strongly to her, right from the beginning. Even though Cheryl was nothing like Iceline to look at—Iceline had been much older, for a start, and very thin, almost dry-looking; and instead of the baggy over-washed T-shirts and wide gathered skirts Cheryl wore, Iceline had dressed every day in a pale grey uniform with a white apron; on her head, a small starched hat, like a paper boat. Iceline had been there in Nancy's parents' Chappaqua home, always. She'd been there before Nancy and her sister Barbara were born and had still been there when they'd left it; moving about the place, like a soft shadow, mopping and polishing and cooking and looking after Nancy and Barbara and keeping everything running smoothly with a stolid, wordless, uncomplaining proficiency. 'That woman,' Nancy's father had been fond of saying (generally about once a week and always within earshot of his vague and dreamy wife), 'is the only thing that stands between this family and Armageddon.'

Nancy, in ten short months, had come to feel the same way about Cheryl. Not that Nancy was vague and dreamy like her mother had been—oh no, certainly not—Nancy thought of everything, Nancy never (unlike her mother) misplaced important things, she was a list-maker, organized and efficient at home and in the office. Even so, she'd come to feel, almost from the first day, that she could never be without Cheryl. The thought of Cheryl ever leaving them was so dreadful she pushed it out of her head every time it popped in there. She loved coming home at the end of the day—always an hour before Beecham even though they worked in the same office building and went in together on the same 7:06 train in the morning, she always came back ahead of him on the 6:20 in the evening so she was home in time to put Bunny to bed—walking, almost running back from the station and leaving the car there for Beecham when he arrived later. She loved stepping into the hallway, everything so neat and clean, everywhere the bright sharp scent of Windex and Soft Scrub and Murphy's Oil Soap, the two of them, Bunny and Cheryl, waiting: Bunny perched on Cheryl's vast swaying hip, newly bathed, in fresh pyjamas, pink and delicious and with his corn-coloured hair parted smartly on the left-hand side so he almost looked like a little boy already instead of a baby still. It was true, it did prick her heart a little, the way he seemed to look older when she came home in the evening than when she'd left him that same morning—subtly different, as if he'd been slowly growing and changing minute by minute and hour by hour while she'd been away from him. But it gave her such joy too, coming back to him, her own boy, her greatest, most miraculous achievement, and such peace, knowing that all the time she was gone he was safe here at home with Cheryl. She couldn't bear the idea of ever having to get someone else in; to have to make Bunny get used to a new girl. It appalled her, the prospect of ever having to limp along, even for a week or two like she'd had to do after the European girl didn't work out and before Mary-Katherine's neighbour had come up with Cheryl; the idea of an agency sitter—a different one each day—rocking up in some battered old Plymouth, Bunny screaming his head off the minute she stepped inside and chucked him under the chin with a curly spangled fingernail.

Which was why she didn't mind that Cheryl didn't do things exactly the way she asked her to do them. It was why she didn't mind that Cheryl kept giving Bunny a bottle when every morning Nancy put out his red sippy cup next to the schedule she'd written out for the day for Cheryl to follow. Or that Cheryl put cereal in Bunny's bottle with his formula. Or that she had the TV on sometimes when Nancy came home in the evening. It was why she turned a blind eye when Cheryl took their best teaspoons to the park to give Bunny his banana instead of the plastic ones that were always left out on the counter next to the fruit bowl in the morning. It was why she voiced no objection when Cheryl purchased Bunny a hideous silky emerald-green sport-shirt with her own money and sometimes dressed him in it instead of in one of the little pastel polo shirts which lay washed and ironed and folded and stacked in two neat piles by Cheryl herself in Bunny's closet in accordance with Nancy's instructions.

Any time Nancy felt herself getting annoyed by any of these things, she told herself that they were not important, not in the great scheme of things. Bunny was happy, Bunny was safe. With all her heart she felt sure of that; that Cheryl would never, ever let any harm come to Bunny, or do anything to make him sad. Cheryl was stubborn about small things, like the spoons and not using the sippy cup; stubborn about doing things her own way, and her English wasn't great and probably she didn't talk to him enough, not as much as you were supposed to talk to a one-year-old, but she was vigilant and careful and very gentle, just like Iceline had been, and when Nancy pictured the future, nothing about it felt to her in any way precarious and Cheryl, in her thin washed-out T-shirts and her bright skirts, was always in it.

Bunny was already sleeping, that last Monday when Nancy arrived home. He lay draped and stretched out like a starfish high up on Cheryl's mountainous shoulder. He was newly-bathed and in his clean pyjamas with his fair hair smartly parted on one side the way it always was when Nancy walked in the door. Cheryl lifted him gently off her shoulder and placed him in Nancy's outstretched arms and then, in her slow imperfect English, she asked if Bunny could go home with her that night and sleep over with her. She'd bring him back in the morning.

Nancy was floored.

She'd never dreamed of Cheryl asking for such a thing. *Bunny, not be here? with them? for a whole night?*

On the table in the hallway she saw that Cheryl had already got ready a supply of Bunny's things to take with her—two clean empty bottles, a tin of formula, four diapers in a Ziploc baggie, a packet of oatmeal cereal, the emerald-green shirt.

Nancy didn't know what to say.

She had a horror, a terror, of offending Cheryl, of making her think she wasn't trusted, of upsetting her so much with a refusal that in the morning she'd announce that she was leaving, she'd found another family to work for, another Bunny to take care of.

Nancy flailed for some sort of practical objection. Where would he sleep? Did Cheryl have a spare bedroom at her place? Did she possess a crib?

A vague picture came into Nancy's mind of a shabby apartment building, a corridor with a door at the end of it, and it occurred to her that she didn't actually know where Cheryl lived. It had always been enough that Cheryl arrived every morning at 6:45 on their doorstep and Nancy was embarrassed now, in the middle of this awkward and unexpected conversation, to ask.

Cheryl said she would make a nest for Bunny on the floor next to her bed out of pillows and blankets.

'Oh I don't know, Cheryl,' said Nancy.

Still holding onto Bunny, she smoothed his soft hair with the palm of her hand and touched his cheek with her finger. 'No,' she said. 'No. I'm sorry, Cheryl, no.'

Cheryl's response was impossible to read. Her broad black face looked the same as always: placid, inscrutable, almost blank.

It's astonishing, really, the things Nancy and Beecham Clay never knew about their babysitter.

The things she never told them and the things they never felt the need to ask about—that her surname was Toussaint for example, and that she lived in a small dark room above the consignment store on Mamaroneck Avenue, and that she was twenty-five years old and had been born in 1975 in the Cité Soleil district of Port-au-Prince and that when she arrived in the United States in 1997 she'd left behind three children of her own.

In a general way of course they understood that Cheryl was here for the money, pure and simple. In a general way they knew this was how things were, and even if they didn't dwell upon the details they probably had a fair idea that at the end of every week when she'd been paid, Cheryl walked out of their house and along Orienta Avenue and turned left onto the Post Road and walked the remaining hundred yards to the A&P where the Western Union counter was and dipped her hand into her cracked plastic purse and took out Nancy's envelope with the dollar bills inside, kept back what she needed for her own rent, and sent the rest home.

That last morning, Nancy was nervy and pale. She'd hardly slept, thinking about Cheryl's unexpected request, worrying about having refused it and yet still feeling she couldn't possibly agree to it. She kept looking at Cheryl as she went round collecting her things for the day—papers, briefcase, laptop, purse, coat—trying to figure out if Cheryl was upset or sulking. It was impossible to tell. Cheryl looked the same as she always did. She looked calm. She looked stolid. She looked heavy and reliable. Nancy hadn't said anything to Beecham about Cheryl wanting to borrow Bunny in case he got worked up about it, in case he said, 'She asked you *what*?' and brought the whole thing up in front of Cheryl while they were getting ready to leave for the station and Cheryl was giving Bunny his breakfast.

Nancy found herself lingering longer than usual, beyond their normal deadline for heading out of the house to the car. She checked and re-checked the contents of her briefcase, her purse. She re-applied her lipstick. She stood looking at Cheryl mashing up Bunny's breakfast banana with a fork. Out in the driveway Beecham leaned on the horn and Nancy, feeling panicky and tearful and strange, wanted to say to Cheryl, 'Please, Cheryl, don't leave us.'

The names of Cheryl's children were Stanley, Webster and Yolisha. Stanley was 8, Webster was 7 and Yolisha was 5 and Cheryl hadn't seen them in four years because if she ever went back home to Haiti to visit them she'd never get back in through immigration again.

'I can't do this,' she'd said to her grandmother on the phone when she first arrived—when she first started housekeeping for Mrs. Landis in New Rochelle.

'How are we going to live, baby, if you don't?' said her grandmother.

In the beginning, when Stanley was 4 and Webster was 3 and Yolisha was 1, she'd talked to her children once a month on the phone, but after the first few months they'd grown too shy to speak to a stranger. All Cheryl could hear when her grandmother put them on the line was their soft breathing and after a time she'd let them be, it seemed too hard a thing for them all.

Which was how, after Mrs. Landis went to live in the retirement home in Phoenix and Cheryl came to work for the Clays, she'd fallen in love with Bunny.

Little by little, she'd started to love him and now she couldn't stop. He had become essential to her. She had so much affection to bestow and her own children were there and Bunny was here and they'd forgotten her and Bunny hadn't and it was such a comfort to have him close, to have him cry for her when she stepped out of the room just for a moment to fetch something and had to sing to him from wherever she was in the house so he could hear her voice and know she was there; that she hadn't left him.

She couldn't help wanting to do things for him the way she'd done them for her own children, like putting cereal in his bottle even though she knew Mrs. Clay didn't like it, or feeding him with the silver spoons from the velvet canteen in the dining room because they had a pattern of three small clubs like on a pack of cards and at home in Port-au-Prince they had a metal spoon that had just that same pattern on it that Stanley had liked to chew on when he had a tooth coming, the cold metal on his hot gums.

She couldn't help wanting to dress Bunny in the soft green sport-shirt she'd bought him instead of in the collared cotton tops he was supposed to wear. It was what she'd have dressed him in if he'd been hers. She hated the collared cotton tops, it was like dressing him in a cardboard box. It made her feel guilty, the nine dollars she'd spent to buy Bunny the shirt instead of sending every last cent home to her grandmother and Stanley and Webster and Yolisha, but the truth was she felt like she loved Bunny now as much as she loved her own children and sometimes it seemed to her that she loved him even more than she loved them. It made her feel guilty but she couldn't help it, and having lost her own children, it seemed to Cheryl that she could never, now, be made to give up Bunny. Having Bunny close did so much to fill up the big empty space in her heart that when 7:30 came round in the evening and Mrs. Clay came bursting in through the door and she had to hand Bunny over and say goodbye she could hardly stand it. He was the only thing that made it possible for her to do this, to live this way.

Out in the driveway Beecham leaned again on the horn and Nancy, finally, picked up her briefcase and her coat and her big leather purse. She kissed Bunny. She breathed in his sweet milky perfume and gave Cheryl her biggest warmest smile and told them both to have a great day and then she left.

In the kitchen, Cheryl put Bunny in his high chair with a rice cake and took out the trash. She emptied the coffee filter and wiped down the machine and put the butter and the milk and the big carton of juice back in the fridge and ran the dishes under warm water and placed them in the dishwasher. She wiped Bunny's face and hands and lifted him up out of his high chair and tickled his belly and kissed his soft corn-coloured hair and tipped him upside down till he chortled and squealed with pleasure and told him he was her Big Boy and then she took him onto the couch where they snuggled up to watch a little early morning television and then she took him upstairs for his morning nap. It always amazed her, how he could be so sleepy so soon after he woke up. None of her own children had ever been like that. Today it was barely nine thirty and Bunny was already sucking his thumb and drifting off.

She settled him in his crib, stood over him, singing and murmuring to him until his eyes closed and his wet thumb had fallen out of his mouth. She told herself not to think about yesterday and Mrs. Clay saying she couldn't keep him for the night. Softly, she closed his door and came back downstairs and went into the basement and put on a load of laundry and came back up into the kitchen and ironed the bed linen that was waiting from yesterday and then she went back upstairs and made Nancy's and Beecham's bed and checked on Bunny and stood looking at him a while and then she came back down again and went into the den to tidy up and it was on the TV.

It was there the moment she went into the den, the silent puff-and-fall of the buildings. First one, then the other.

And after that, everything a strange kind of dream—

Mr. Clay's brother Robert coming from Rhode Island and staying in the guest bedroom and going into the city every day and coming back in the evenings, grey dust in his hair and in his eyelashes. Mr. Clay's brother Robert going back to Rhode Island. Mrs. Clay's sister Barbara and her husband arriving from Madison, Wisconsin, Mrs. Clay's sister hugging Cheryl, the two of them crying in each other's arms.

All the packing. Mrs. Clay's sister saying the journey back would take them sixteen hours.

Cheryl thinking that 'them' meant her too. Their big blue car, leaving. His golden head.

Cheryl standing in front of the Clays' locked house, then walking slowly along the curving tree-lined avenue down to the Post Road and turning right towards the harbour. The masts of the boats tinkling softly against each other, the harbour water dark and still.

Stanley, Webster and Yolisha looking out at her from behind a plastic window in her wallet, remote and unfamiliar. She still had Bunny's smell with her, in her clothes and in her skin, his warm cereal perfume. She still had his sturdy weight in her lap, his sleeping cheek in the hollow above her collarbone. She counted the money she had left from her last week's wages, seventeen dollars and some change. She put the change in the pocket of her skirt and folded the bills and tucked them back in her wallet behind her children. Overhead a plane dropped down into the re-opened airport, then another and another and another, their lights bright in the sky.

In the morning she'd start looking for a new family.

MIRACLE AT HAWK'S BAY

MATTHEW HIGH. WE knew it would be him. Even before Hannah turned him over, we just knew it.

It was Annie who saw him from the road. 'Look,' she said, and when she pointed at the dark shape out there in the shallow water, there was only one thought in all our heads—please God, let it not be him. Let it be any of the others but not him, not Matthew High.

At the beginning of the marshes we took off our boots and our stockings and hitched up our skirts and ran along the high grassy mounds above the channels, hopping over the gaps where you could hear the creep of the tide trickling in and filling them up. He was out on the sand, and even though we all knew it would be Matthew, when we were quite close Annie said, 'Who is it?' because the truth was we couldn't tell for sure. Even then, from the look and shape of him, all blobby and blown-up, it might have been someone else. He was lying on his front in just a shirt which was up over his head in a sodden lump of cloth. We went towards him through the shallow water and stood

79

around him like a kind of crescent moon with our backs to the sea, and I remember feeling the water lapping at my heels, thinking that if we all stood aside now and went back the way we'd come the water would rise and cover him again and take him back and Bella High would never have to know. I looked at Annie and Hannah to see if they were thinking the same thing but I couldn't tell. Their eyes were down, looking at the dark and swollen body of Matthew High.

Hannah stepped forward and took hold of the soggy mound of cloth at his head and squeezed it. She wrung it out and smoothed it down a little way and when Annie helped her turn him over the two of them pulled smartly at the filthy hem to cover his naked parts. His face was the colour of a thunder cloud, and one of his eyes was gone. There was a wound in the ugly swelling of his ankles, a slice of his soft flesh beginning to uncurl from around the bone, like the peel from an orange. White sea-lice crawled in the open seam. Hannah knelt beside him and put her arm behind his neck and tried to raise him but she couldn't move him. He was half sunk down in the wet sand and even when we lifted the hanks of his long hair so there was nothing holding him down, we couldn't shift his weight, only roll him to and fro. So Hannah took his arms and Annie and I took his feet and we tried again but we still couldn't move him. It was like trying to drag a hammock full of stones. I wondered if we might have to leave him after all, but Hannah said we should probably bring a door and put him on that; wait for him to float up with the rising

water and float him to the shore and carry him home to
Bella on the door.

She looked at Annie and asked her if she'd go with
her and help her take the door off its hinges at the back
of her place and bring it down, but Annie was staring at
Matthew and biting her thumb and didn't seem to know
how to answer, so Hannah turned to me instead.

'Peggy,' she said. 'We have to.'

'Do we?' I said.

'Yes,' said Hannah, in a firm voice, so I said all right
I'd go with her if she wanted me to, but wouldn't it be
better if I stayed behind with Annie to hold him while the
tide came in? If there weren't two of us to hold him when
he floated up out of the sand we might lose him again.

Hannah seemed to think about this, and for a moment
I thought she was going to say, *Well perhaps that would
be for the best, if we lost him again*, but she didn't, what
she said was that she'd go back by herself for the door and
collect Mary on the way to help.

So Hannah went off to fetch Mary and the door and
Annie stayed behind with me and while they were gone
Matthew High rose up slowly out of the muddy sand on
the incoming tide. We took a hand and a foot each, Annie
and I, and held him there while he rocked back and forth
on the surface of the rising water. I looked at Annie. She
was thinking about Bella, you could tell.

'They will have to hurry,' she said.

'Yes,' I said, 'They will.'

You have to see the tide here to believe it: once it starts
properly on its way—once it's finished its long slow trickling

start—it comes racing forward in a great greedy rush, and even floating in the water Matthew High was heavy and hard to hold onto and kept sinking down beneath the surface. I kept looking at Annie. I knew what she was thinking because I was thinking it too—that we could both of us let go of his hands and feet and leave him there till the tide turned and let him ride back out on it like a Viking and be dragged down by the current; the sea would take him and Bella would never know. I think there was a part in all of us that day that was tempted, even Hannah, and while I stood there in the freezing water with Annie Cotton, I thought, *well, if they are too long we will just have to let go and that will be that and no one could ever blame us*. Faster and faster the water rose up around our waists and our skirts swirled around us like weed on top of the grey water and so did Matthew High's long thick hair. He lay between us like a big puffy eiderdown. There was a weight to him though, even in the water, a gravity. He was swollen and cold but he was so solid it made you want to cry out. I thought of Bella and I wanted more than anything to let him go, but we could see the others now, coming back with the door, Hannah trotting smartly in front, Mary behind.

'Look,' said Annie suddenly for the second time that day, and this time she was pointing to a shell, lodged in the mucky hollow where Matthew's missing eye had been. It was small and white and shaped like a helter-skelter. I picked it out and closed my hand around it and pressed its point into my palm to feel the sharpness of the pain.

When Hannah and Mary came splashing towards us we pulled Bella's husband to them and when we had him on the door we floated him to the shore and carried him over the grassy mounds between the channels and laid him on the shingle between the marshes and the road and that was when we saw Bella High heading along the road in her rubber boots and her long jumper and her yellow skirt.

Even from this far off, it was obvious she didn't know yet. You could tell by her walk that she hadn't seen anything.

'You go and tell her Peggy,' said the others but I said I couldn't do it. I knew I couldn't be the one to tell her. I knew the words would lodge in my throat like a splint of wood and I would stand there looking at Bella High's lovely face with its sparkling grey eyes and its sweet mouth and all those glossy chestnut curls falling over her shoulders like a shower of bells and I knew I didn't have the strength for it. I knew I wouldn't be able to drag the words up. They would stay there like a big clot, or a hard pebble, stuck in the narrow tightness at the dark back of my mouth. You could tell none of the others wanted to do it either. No one had the stomach for it, not even Hannah, not really. Annie looked at her feet. They were cold and dirty and covered in black sand. She was shivering. Mary was gawping at the bloated mound of Matthew stretched out upon the door.

At last Hannah said, all right she would go. She would go home and put on her mourning bonnet and then she would go to Bella High's house and tell her to prepare for a funeral and then the rest of us could bring Matthew to her.

We watched as Hannah set off towards the road above the shingle beach and Bella, further up, carried on along it in her yellow skirt. Moving against the stone walls and the dark gorse at the road's edge she looked like a piece of sunlight or a daffodil petal or a rich curl of fresh butter, and I felt a kind of burning in my chest, looking at Matthew lying with his flabby upturned face upon the door.

She was at her gate with Hannah when we came up to the house, her hand to her mouth. There'd been such a tension among us, all the way—me and Annie and Mary—carrying him back, all of us silent, getting ready to show him to her. I can still feel it, the weight of him on the door, the huge squashy bulk of him, like a vast fish or a great dense jelly, the way he flopped and bounced.

Matthew High, here. Matthew High home. Returned, delivered.

She was quiet, Bella. None of us knew what to say to her. When Hannah said, 'Will we bring him in, Bella?' she just nodded. She looked small like a child and I felt huge and big-knuckled and ugly the way all of us always do in the presence of Bella High. When we brought him in on the door Mary said, 'Where will we put him?' and Bella said, 'On the bed,' and until that moment when we rolled him off the door onto the bed in a big squidgy lump, dripping slime and water onto the counterpane and the wide clean boards of Bella High's floor, she had not shed a tear but when she saw him lying on their bed she started shaking and gulping and none of us knew what to do and it seemed like it would go on forever, her weeping and us standing there like a row of posts but in the end Hannah stepped over to her and put her arms around her and said, 'Hush.

You must get him ready,' and when at last Bella was quiet again she went to the dresser and opened a drawer and pulled out a cloth and a comb and began to wash and dry him. She rubbed his long hair with the cloth and pulled the teeth of the comb through it, pushing the water up and out, tugging gently when it caught on a shell or a snail or a frill of slimy weed. She made a kind of topknot behind his head, which was how he used to wear it and when she was done we watched as she kissed the bony hollow with its lost eye and took the blotched pumpkin face between her hands and held it, cupping it close, like a piece of treasure.

I tried to picture myself in my own home, holding a cloth and a comb, fetching a folded suit and a white laundered shirt from the dresser and saying, as she was now, to Annie and Mary and Hannah and me, *Pass me that necktie will you, those socks and shoes? Help me, will you please, while I get my husband into these?*

A little while later, Elizabeth Lesh came, and Fran Hodge, and the Cragg sisters. The news had spread quickly and by nightfall there was no one who hadn't come to witness it, this offering from the sea.

It is the worst of all sins, envy. It eats away at what's left of your heart and fills you up with black and bitter thoughts and shrinks your life to nothing, and it isn't because you've been *told* that envy is a terrible ugly sin that you know it to be true—not like other sins that you're told are wrong but don't feel it—it's because you can *feel* the way this one eats you up and shrivels your whole life until you're nothing but a dry envious stick with nothing in your soul but the thought of Bella High and her vast tremendous luck; her great good fortune.

It was Annie who broke down, just as we were getting ready to leave the house; poor scrawny boss-eyed Annie who went up to Bella High and started screaming in her face that it wasn't fair, the way she was always the one to get everything in this life—how it had always been her that was blessed with the best of everything and now it was the same all over again and Annie held out her long empty hands before Bella High and shook them and wheeled round in front of us and shouted to us all as if we didn't know it, that the earth was a place of gifts for Bella High, always had been. Everything she wanted it gave up to her in the end. She had always had the earth's gifts and now she had the sea's too.

'Come, Annie,' said Hannah at last and stepped forward and took hold of Annie's stringy red wrists and pulled her away and said to all of us that we should go now. So we all went home to fetch our funeral bonnets and came back and with Bella helping this time, we gathered Matthew up onto the door again and carried him to the church and Mary conducted the service and when he was buried we all left Bella with him. At the gate I turned and saw that she had lain down on top of the earth, and perhaps you will tell me that it would make no difference to be able to do that but it seems to me that it would.

She has put up a small round stone since then and she visits it often, this firm spot on the earth where she has laid him to rest.

When it was all over we took off our funeral bonnets and put them away. We all knew we would not need them again. It is something to do with the current here, the particular way it bends its muscle around this piece of shore. It means that when a boat goes over and is pulled down the men are flushed away and we do not see them again, ever.

Even so, a few of us went down afterwards to the shore and stood next to the little pile of greasy flotsam we have salvaged over the years that is ours—the orange buoy, the square of green nylon netting, the spars of wood, the shadows on the water that are nothing but the clouds.

IN THE CABIN IN THE WOODS

ON FRIDAYS WHEN we met in the cave above the weir after school I always brought Trude something—some chocolates or some leftover wine I'd smuggled out of the house or a few flowers from the garden Mutti wouldn't miss—and in exchange she would give me a kiss. But after a few weeks my little gifts began to get on her nerves and one afternoon towards the end of autumn when I arrived with a handful of marigolds, she told me she was bored of my presents and the only thing she could think of that was interesting enough for her to want me to bring it to her, the only thing she could think of I could give her that would ever persuade her to kiss me again, was the heart of Magdalena Hirsch.

From this I concluded that she was bored of me, that she didn't really want to see me anymore, and this was her way of telling me to get lost. I went home, throwing the marigolds in the river on the way and told myself I'd better forget about Trude.

But I couldn't. Trude's lips were so soft and warm and kissing her in the cool cave after school was the best thing

I'd ever done. I kept thinking about her and I kept thinking about what she'd said about bringing her the heart of Magdalena Hirsch. It was a stupid thing, I knew it was, but somehow it caught hold of my imagination and wouldn't let it go and in the end one evening when supper was over and the washing up was done and everything was put away in its proper place, and Vati had settled down in front of the TV with his newspaper and his pipe, I told Mutti I was going over to Dieter's for an hour or so and I'd be back later and then I set off in the direction of the Hauptallee and from there I made my way to the cinder path that led into the woods.

'Don't be too long, Peter,' Mutti called after me.

'I won't.'

I'd never been near Magdalena's cabin in my whole life. I had no idea where to head for. I'd been into the woods many times to pick blackberries and elderflower and to take our old dachshund, Lili, for walks, but in my whole life I'd never gone beyond the point where the cinder path stopped and the dense middle part of the woods began. I don't know how long I walked through the thick wood. It was dark and drizzling and even through the trees the drizzle came down onto my face and hands.

When I came to it there was no clearing and no garden, only a low wall that ran round the cabin; no gate in the wall, just an opening you had to walk through to get to the door. I knocked but there was no reply.

It was years since I'd thought about Magdalena Hirsch, let alone seen her, and I'd never heard of anyone ever coming out here to visit her.

I walked into a small sitting room with bare timbered walls, a plain wooden table and a single chair next to it. On the floorboards lay striped woven rugs, the kind people like my Oma used to make during the war out of torn-up rags. In the corner there was a fireplace with a neat pile of logs next to it, a scattering of ash and cinders in the grate. There was a bed, cupboards and pans that hung from hooks in the ceiling; an oblong sink on cast iron legs. In the sink there was a plate sprinkled with crumbs, a knife smeared with butter. A little water had been run on top of the plate and some of the crumbs were floating in it. The bed was neatly made and covered from head to foot with a rough wool blanket. Beneath the blanket, when I lifted it, I found her pillow in a white cotton slip, small and flat and square; a flowery eiderdown, silky and cold. On the wall there was a bamboo mirror with a narrow dresser beneath it and on top of the dresser there was a white cloth and on top of the cloth there was a black lacquered box with a lid, oval in shape and roughly the size of my fist.

I have taken out my heart and put it in a box where no more harm can ever come to it.

Magdalena's words had terrified us all when we were children. The thought of her warm wet heart in its chilly little box, fluttering and beating beneath the lid like some small, frightened animal—it was like something out of Grimm.

Every once in a while, she came into town for something—a bag of tea from Gephardts' or a ball of wool from Greta Fahr's shop, matches or fuel from Dortmund's—and always at some point she'd alight on someone, Greta Fahr or Herr Gephardt or one of the Dortmund girls or one of our mothers if they happened to be in any of those places when she was there, and she would tell them in a confidential whisper what she'd done and sometimes, crouching down in her old black coat and her long skirt and her funny smock, she'd confide in one of us children as well.

We used to wonder what had made her do it, but she never told us that part. Whatever it was that had happened to her she'd never spoken about it. There was no gossip, no rumours or stories. Whatever it was, it was buried in some dark place, as secret and hidden as the heart she said she'd pulled from her body and locked away, out of sight and out of mind, and when we'd asked our parents, or Herr Gephardt or Fräulein Fahr, or any of the other grown-ups if they knew, they just shrugged and shook their heads and said she was just a poor creature who should have gone years ago to the hospital in Euskirchen where she could be looked after instead of living out in the woods in that little cabin by herself.

I didn't hear her come in.

I didn't hear her set down the logs on the floor next to the hearth, I didn't hear her step onto the woven rug and walk up behind me. I didn't know she was there until we were standing together in front of the mirror, the two of us, me in front and her behind, me and Magdalena Hirsch.

I had never seen her up close before and it was ages since I'd seen her in town; years since I'd happened to be there when she'd paid one of her rare visits to the shops in the Hauptallee. She looked, to me, neither young nor old.

She was slender and tall and her brownish-greyish hair was very straight and soft-looking. Her eyes were grey and the skin of her face was pale from living in the woods. She still had on her black coat from being outside but the buttons at the front were open and I could see her smock underneath. It was dark and rough looking and loosely woven and hung in folds from her shoulders and behind the folds I could see her shape. I thought of Trude. Trude with her starched white blouse and her straw-coloured plaits and the stingy kisses she'd sold to me in the cave above the weir. My face had grown suddenly very hot, I could see it in the mirror, red and burning beneath my short dark hair that was still damp from the rain. Behind us I could see the bed, the white pillow and the flowery eiderdown that had been cold when I'd touched it, and I could feel Magdalena's breath, very quick and warm on the back of my neck. She smelled of milk and woodsmoke.

'You?' she whispered, bewildered, amazed.

A rose-coloured flush had spread into her waxy face and her mouth was open. I didn't know what to say. Her eyes were wide and her face was taut and very still and she was staring into the bamboo mirror at my reflection as if she had seen a ghost. I swallowed and waited and she said it again—*You?*—and then her arms came up around me and quick as snake she reached past me to the dresser and snatched up the little fist-sized box that was on top of the cloth and sprang away from me.

'Get out,' she said softly, clutching the shiny black container against her open coat, hugging it and pressing down with her thumbs on its lacquered lid as if her life depended on it, and then her voice rose and she shouted at me at the top of her lungs, to get away from her, right now, and never come back, to go back through the woods the way I'd come, back to my wife and my baby son, she didn't want to see me ever again, she didn't need me anymore, everything was fine now just the way it was and if I ever tried coming back to her ever again, she would kill me.

THE COAT

SOMETIMES WHEN I arrived she'd open the front door and just stand there as if she'd hardly noticed I'd come— her arms folded beneath her breasts, watching the empty battered garment fill with the breeze from the open door, the body swelling up and moving about, as if it were alive. I wondered if she took it down at night from its curved hook, put its soft arms around her neck, its hips against her hips, and danced with it across the room and told it she loved it.

In the evenings, when I sat with her in the lamplight, I could see it out there, hanging in the passageway. The three scuffed leather buttons down one side, the nub of thick pewtery thread where a fourth had gone missing. It made me think of a roughed-up dog after a fight.

'You should fold it away, Evangelina,' I'd say then, as gently as I could. 'Pack it up with your memories and put everything in a box and start again.'

When she didn't say anything I'd reach out and cover her hand with mine.

'Forget him, Evangelina.'

'No.'

It was grey, a soft dark grey like old heather or the sea at Duddon in winter. Broad-shouldered and long-armed like Joseph himself. She kept it on a hook next to the front door like some kind of charm, a lure that would bring him home, like one of the lamps in the windows of the inn that were there to guide the carts and carriages safely across the bay.

It was more than a year since Joseph Hine had walked out of the door and left without a word of goodbye or explanation of any kind and Evangelina kept dreaming up all kinds of reasons why he might have gone. Once, in a flood of tears, she asked me if I thought there might be some far-off war she'd never heard of he'd felt called upon to fight; another time, if I thought it could have been something religious, some difficult question to do with his soul he'd gone away to figure out.

'Don't be daft,' I wanted to say.

I don't think it ever entered her head, what everyone thought: that her good-looking husband must have another woman somewhere, in Blackpool or Manchester or Liverpool. Somewhere glamorous and busy she'd never been, someone Joseph had met when he went off carousing three times a year with his uncles and his brothers and his sisters' big loud-mouthed husbands.

Once, not long after he took himself off, there'd been a report of a horse out on the sands with its saddle hanging down under its belly and the body of a man trailing beneath. Sonny Peen had seen it from his little hut above the shore and come running into town making frantic shapes with his arms and bellowing from his long wordless mouth. Sonny always liked to be the first with news of anything interesting or unusual out in the bay and when Evangelina heard his awful bellowing—that terrible donkey-sound of his that was like an ancient seesaw, or the slow drawing up of a bucket on a rusty winch from the bottom of a cavernous well—when she heard it she went running down there with a shawl pulled on over her nightgown but it wasn't Joseph it was only a poor traveller attempting to cross over in the dark without a guide. Since then there'd been nothing, no rumours or sightings or reports or false alarms; Evangelina the only person who didn't believe that the emptiness out in the bay, the mist, and the water creeping soundlessly back and forth beneath the moon, in and out over the sands, were the silence of a man who was doing his best to disappear.

It was the minister at Bethesda who first asked me to visit Evangelina, to sit with her from time to time and keep her company.

'It will do her good, Margaret,' he said, 'to have someone there. Another voice, another face.'

We all knew by then what had happened when the schoolteacher, Mr. Gardiner, had gone to visit her in his best clothes with a bunch of snowdrops in his fist.

'Are you blind?' she'd shouted at him from the open doorway, not even asking him across the threshold, and pointing at Joseph's coat. She snatched hold of one tattered grey lapel and shook it in the schoolteacher's face. Didn't he know she was waiting for her husband to come home? Couldn't he see that? Her voice shrill, indignant, amazed. The schoolteacher blushed, he was young like she was and thirteen months must have seemed a long time to him for a good-looking husband to be gone and for his wife to believe he was ever coming back. When she carried on shouting at him he dropped his flowers and hastened backwards down the path. He hadn't argued with her. If that's what she wanted to believe, he'd told people afterwards, let her.

We didn't talk much, Evangelina and I, and hardly ever, after those first few months, about Joseph.

We sat, we sorted laundry, we quartered fruit and cooked it and packed it in jars. We walked, we planted out her garden for winter—onions and kale and some pale flat wrinkled beans I'd never seen which she said wouldn't mind the frost and would be soft and tender and delicious by early summer, and I remember thinking that it was a good sign, that she was talking about the summer as if she looked forward to it, and a picture came into my head then of me and Evangelina Hine sitting down to a plate of new beans on a table in her garden in summer. Later, too, another picture came: in my mind, winter has always appeared like a big, dark shoulder, or the long curve of a road up ahead, and once you are round it, it is all downhill and I remember standing on the ridged earth in Evangelina's garden between her quiet house and Joseph's empty forge behind it, seeing the two of us, me and Evangelina Hine on a sledge, in the last of the winter's snows, somewhere up on the fells, Evangelina clinging on tightly behind, our heels stuck out to the side, our toes pointing up, hurtling down, shrieking and crying out and laughing.

I began to hate the stupid coat. The way she clung to it, its woollen crust. Its grey shell. All her hopes crowded into it, all her passion and all her faith, as if just by hanging there, all limp and droopy and old, it was some kind of promise or pledge, a sign that he would come back to her one day, warm and safe and whole.

I made up my mind to tell her what I thought, what everyone thought, about Joseph having another sweetheart somewhere and her being too blind to see it.

'Evangelina,' I began slowly, but there must have been something in my voice that suggested I was about to say something she didn't want to hear. She was sitting opposite me at her kitchen table, peeling the apples we'd brought in from the shed behind the forge where we'd stored them in the autumn. I thought how thin and tired she looked.

'What?' she said, keeping her eyes down. I watched while she picked up a fresh apple and dug the blade of her knife into its wrinkled skin and carried on, more briskly and fiercely than before. She had never looked so stubborn. She began dumping the peeled apples into a pan and drawing the loose peel together into a mound between her hands.

'Perhaps, Evangelina—' I began, but she cut me off.

'How is Harold?' she said, in a bright way.

I took a breath.

'Harold is fine,' I said. 'Busy at the bank.'

Harold is fine, I wanted to say, but he is not you.

Harold and I lived then, as we do now, in a large house in the village, a half mile walk to Evangelina's place. Being the forge, hers is the last of all the houses and beyond it is open country and the sea. I always loved that walk to her house, once in the morning, and then again in the early evening, when I said goodbye to Harold and set off from our house to see her. The water and the big sky and the hills rising behind.

Harold would always ask me, when I came home after my visits how 'the poor woman' was. He would always say how good I was to keep going there and spending so much time with her. Then he would kiss me on my forehead and pat my hand and tell me some story from the bank.

Spring came and in Evangelina's garden we put in peas and raspberries and potatoes, a quince against the wall at the back of the house. The beans were getting so tall we had to support them with ropes strung between pairs of stakes, one at either end of each row.

It was Sonny Peen who saw Joseph Hine walking back across the bay.

Harold and I were away.

The Ulverston bank had closed for a day's holiday and Harold had arranged a trip to Maryport. It seems foolish now, but as we walked about through the streets and around the harbour and sat over our lunch in the Golden

Lion, I actually found myself looking out for Joseph Hine to see if this might be where he'd decided in the end to begin his new life away from Evangelina. It seems foolish now, in view of everything that has happened, that in a kiosk near the harbour wall, I bought Evangelina a china thimble with *A Present From Maryport* written along the bottom in tiny blue script.

Sonny Peen's wooden hut is perched on the rock above the shore, something like the lookout on a rampart. It has a chimney made of beaten metal, one small window at the front made of pieces of bottle-glass stuck inside a shellacked frame. From there he can see all comers, which is what he likes. He likes to see the travellers coming in when the tide is chasing them, when they have to cluster around the guide's white horse and cling to the edges of his floating cloak, like rats on a cheese. He likes to see the shapes of the people and the carts and the carriages looming up through the mist like creatures from the deep, and when he spots something out in the bay he makes a circle with his forefinger and his thumb, as if he has a telescope, and then he presses his good eye to the imaginary glass and closes the other eye and squints through the hole. He does this several times a day, and, depending on whether the tide is in or out, he sees carts and carriages and wading birds, herons and egrets picking their way delicately through the muddy sand; fishing boats and seagulls afloat on the rocking grey surface of the water.

Perhaps Sonny had his own theory all along about what had happened to Joseph Hine; perhaps he'd studied the big blacksmith from afar through his make-believe telescope and perceived some unusual sort of anguish; perhaps it had seemed to him that Evangelina's husband was not well, that he was suffering or sickening for something and had gone away, like a cat or an elephant, to die. Perhaps, when Sonny Peen spied the tall powerful figure of Joseph Hine approaching across the shimmering sand, and saw his long weird clothing, snapping and guttering in the salt wind, he thought he was looking at a shroud.

But when Joseph Hine came back, he wasn't a ghost. When Joseph Hine stepped off the wet sand into the marshy grass of the foreshore, what Sonny Peen saw, through the small shellacked frame of the bottle-glass window in his little wooden hut, was a woman.

He is a sight, though I suppose most of us are used to it now.

It is more than a year since he returned and I have often wondered what it was like, his first meeting with Evangelina when he came back, the first time he walked in through the door in his woman's clothes. I have often imagined their conversation.

Joseph?

Evangelina.

A long silence.

How are you?

I don't know. I missed you. I wanted to come home.

Another long silence.

I kept your coat for you.

Thank you. Thank you, Evangelina. That was kind.

Another long silence.
Joseph?
Yes?
Come.

When they are out in cold weather Joseph wears the big grey coat on top of his woman's clothes.

For the forge he has his old apron as before, and though there are some, like Harold, who have chosen to take their business elsewhere, he appears to manage—he is still good, I suppose, at what he does.

It is hard to say exactly what he has become.

Underneath it all, it seems, he is still a man for they have a child now, the two of them—a little girl called May, and there is every appearance of Evangelina having another one on the way.

I have kept the china thimble I bought for her in Maryport and I would like, if I could, to give it to her, but Harold has forbidden it. He grows sweaty and uneasy if he ever finds himself within a hundred yards of Joseph Hine, coat or no coat. If he sees them in the street, Joseph and Evangelina and their little girl, he grips my arm firmly behind the elbow and marches us over to the other side.

In the evenings I watch him across the table, chewing on his dinner, the bones of his face moving and clicking at his temples, and from time to time he'll look up at me and nod, and with his mouth full and food brimming onto his whiskers, he'll say how good the dinner is, how tasty the meat, and afterwards, later, when we have drunk our tea and read a few pages out of our books or the newspaper and he is busy doing his thing above me in the dark, I'll think about being high up on the fell with Evangelina in the last of the winter's snows, her cheek against my neck, her arms across my heart.

THE REDEMPTION OF GALEN PIKE

THEY'D ALL SEEN Sheriff Nye bringing Pike into town: the two shapes snaking down the path off the mountain through the patches of melting snow and over the green showing beneath, each of them growing bigger as they moved across the rocky pasture and came down into North Street to the jailhouse—Nye on his horse, the tall gaunt figure of Galen Pike following behind on the rope.

The current Piper City jailhouse was a low cramped brick building containing a single square cell, Piper City being at this time, in spite of the pretensions of its name, a small and thinly populated town of a hundred and ninety-three souls in the foothills of the Colorado mountains. Aside from the cell, there was a scrubby yard behind, where the hangings took place, a front office with a table, a chair and a broom; a hook on the wall where the cell keys hung from a thick ring; a small stove where Knapp the jailer warmed his coffee and cooked his pancakes in the morning.

For years, Walter Haig's sister Patience had been visiting the felons who found themselves incarcerated for any length of time in the Piper City jail. Mostly they were outsiders—drifters and vagrants drawn to the place by the occasional but persistent rumours of gold—and whenever one came along, Patience visited him.

Galen Pike's crime revolted Patience more than she could say, and on her way to the jailhouse to meet him for the first time, she told herself she wouldn't think of it; walking past the closed bank, the shuttered front of the general store, the locked-up haberdasher's, the drawn blinds of the dentist, she averted her gaze.

She would do what she always did with the felons; she would bring Galen Pike something to eat and drink, she would sit with him and talk to him and keep him company in the days that he had left. She would not recite scripture, or lecture him about the Commandments or the deadly sins, and she would only read to him if he desired it—a psalm or a prayer or a few selected verses she thought might be helpful to someone in his situation but that was all.

She was a thin, plain woman, Patience Haig.

Straight brown hair scraped back from her forehead so severely that there was a small bald patch where the hair was divided in the centre. It was tied behind in a long dry braid. Her face, too, was long and narrow, her features small and unremarkable, except for her nose which was damaged and lopsided, the right nostril squashed and flattened against the bridge. She wore black flat-heeled boots and a grey dress with long sleeves and a capacious square collar. She was thirty-six years old.

If the preparation of the heart is taken seriously the right words will come. As she walked, Patience silently repeated the advice Abigail Warner had given her when she'd passed on to Patience the responsibility of visiting the jail. Patience was always a little nervous before meeting a new prisoner for the first time, and as she came to the end of Franklin Street and turned the corner into North, she reminded herself that the old woman's advice had always stood her in good stead: if she thought about how lonely it would be—how bleak and frightening and uncomfortable—to be shut up in a twelve-foot box far from home without company or kindness, then whatever the awfulness of the crime that had been committed, she always found that she was able, with the help of her basket of biscuits and strawberry cordial, to establish a calm and companionable atmosphere in the grim little room. Almost always, she had found the men happy to see her.

'Good morning, Mr. Pike,' she said, stepping through the barred door and hearing it clang behind her.

Galen Pike loosened the phlegm in his scrawny throat, blew out his hollow cheeks and hawked on the ground.

'I have warm biscuits,' continued Patience, setting her basket on the narrow table between them, 'and strawberry cordial.'

Pike looked her slowly up and down. He looked at her flat-heeled tightly-laced boots, her grey long-sleeved dress and scraped-back hair and asked her, in a nasty smoke-cracked drawl, if she was a preacher.

'No,' said Patience, 'I am your friend.'

Pike burst out laughing.

He bared his yellow teeth and threw back his mane of filthy black hair and observed that if she was his friend she'd have brought him something a little stronger than strawberry cordial to drink.

If she was his friend, he said, lowering his voice and pushing his vicious ravenous-looking face close to hers and rocking forward on the straight-backed chair to which he was trussed with rope and a heavy chain, she'd have used her little white hand to slip the key to his cell off its hook on her way in and popped it in her pretty Red Riding Hood basket instead of leaving it out there on the goddamn wall with that fat pancake-scoffing fucker of a jailer.

Patience blinked and took a breath and replied crisply that he should know very well she couldn't do the second thing, and she certainly wouldn't do the first because she didn't believe anyone needed anything stronger than strawberry cordial to refresh themselves on a warm day.

She removed the clean white cloth that covered the biscuits. The cloth was damp from the steam and she used it to wipe the surface of the greasy little table which was spotted and streaked with thick unidentifiable stains, and poured out three inches of cordial into the pewter mug she'd brought from home that belonged to her brother Walter.

She told Galen Pike that she would sit with him; that she would come every morning between now and Wednesday unless he told her not to, and on Wednesday she would come too, to be with him then also, if he desired it. In the meantime, if he wanted to, he could unburden himself about what he had done, she would not judge him. Or they could talk about other things, or if he liked she would read to him, or they might sit in silence if he preferred. She didn't mind in the least, she said, if they sat in silence, she was used to silence, she liked it almost more than speaking.

Pike looked at her, frowning and wrinkling his big hooked nose, as if he was trying to figure out whether he'd been sent a mad person. When he didn't make any reply to what she'd said, Patience settled herself in the chair opposite him and took out her knitting and for half an hour neither she nor Galen Pike spoke a word, until Pike, irritated perhaps by the prolonged quiet or the rapid clickety-clack of her wooden needles, leaned across the table with the top half of his scrawny body and twisted his face up close to hers like before and asked, what was a dried-up old lady like her doing knitting a baby's bootie?

Patience coloured at the insult but ignored it and told Pike that she and the other women from the Franklin Street Friends' Meeting House were preparing a supply of clothing for Piper City's new hostel for unwed mothers. A lot of girls, she said, ended up coming this way, dragging themselves along the Boulder Road, looking for somewhere to lay their head.

Pike slouched against the back of his chair. He twisted his grimy-fingered hands which were fastened together in a complicated knot and roped tightly, one on top of the other, across his lap.

'Unwed mothers?' he said in a leering unpleasant way. 'Where all is that then?'

'Nowhere at present,' Patience replied, looking up from her work, 'but when it opens it will be here on North Street. The application is with the mayor.'

When Patience Haig wasn't visiting the occasional residents of the Piper City jail, she was fighting the town's Republican mayor, Byron Lym.

Over the years, she and her brother Walter and the other Friends from the Franklin Street Meeting House had joined forces with the pastor and congregation of the Episcopalian church and a number of other Piper City residents to press for certain improvements in the town: a new roof for the dilapidated schoolhouse; a road out to Piet Larsen's so they could get a cart out there from time to time and bring the old man into town so he could feel a bit of life about him; a library; a small fever hospital; a hostel on North Street for unwed mothers.

So far, Lym had blocked or sabotaged each and every one of the projects. He'd said no to the new roof for the school, no to Piet Larsen's road, no to the library, no to the hospital and a few days from now, they would find out if he was going to say no to the hostel too.

'He is a difficult man, the mayor,' said Patience, but Pike wasn't listening, he was looking out through the cell's tiny window at the maroon peaks of the mountains and when, at the end of an hour, he had asked no more questions about the hostel or anything else, or shown any desire at all to enter into any kind of conversation, Patience put her needles together and placed the finished bootie in her basket and told him that she would come again in the morning if he'd like her to.

Pike yawned and without turning his eyes from the window told her to suit herself, it was all the same to him whether she came or not. In another week he would be dead and that would be that.

Over the next three days, Patience visited Galen Pike every morning.

She brought fresh biscuits and cordial and asked Pike if he wished to talk, or have her read to him. When he didn't reply she took out her knitting and they sat together in silence.

On the fifth morning, a Sunday, Patience arrived a little later than usual, apologising as she stepped in past Knapp when he unlocked, and then locked, the barred door behind her; she'd been at Meeting for Worship, she said, and there'd been a great quantity of notices afterwards, mostly on the subject of the hostel, as the mayor had indicated he'd be making his decision shortly, possibly as early as tomorrow.

Pike yawned and spat on the floor and said he didn't give a shit where she'd been or what she'd been doing and the only thing he wanted to know was how she'd got that pretty nose.

Knapp, in his office, peeped out from behind his newspaper. He'd never known any of the men to be so unmannerly to Miss Haig. He craned his neck a little farther to see if anything interesting would happen now, if Patience Haig would put Pike in his place, or maybe get up and walk out and leave him to rot in there by hisself for the last three days of his life like he deserved.

'I fell off a gate, Mr. Pike,' said Patience. 'When I was nine.'

'Ain't that a shame,' said Pike in his nasty drawl, and Knapp kept his eye on Patience, but all she said was that it was quite all right she'd got used to it a long time ago and didn't notice it unless people remarked on it, which in her experience they never did unless they meant to be rude or unkind, and after that the two of them settled into their customary silence.

Patience took out her knitting.

In his office Knapp folded up the newspaper and began heating his coffee and cooking his pancakes. The fat in his skillet began to pop and smoke and then he poured in the batter and when the first pancake was cooked he slid it onto a plate and then he cooked another and another and when he had a pile of half a dozen he drew his chair up to his table and began to eat. Every so often he looked up and over into the cell where Patience Haig and Galen Pike sat together, as if he was still hoping for some significant event or exchange of words, something he might tell his wife about on Wednesday when he was done keeping an eye on Pike and could go home. It was creepy, he thought, as he munched on his pancakes and gulped his coffee, the way the fellow was so scrawny and thin.

'*QUIT SNOOPING*!' yelled Pike all of a sudden into the silence, opening his mouth wide in a big yellow-toothed snarl that made Knapp jump like a frightened squirrel and drop his fork.

'Jesus Christ,' growled Pike. 'Nosy fat curly-tailed fuckin' hog.'

He turned to Patience. 'What all d'y'all do then? At the worship meeting?'

Patience laid down her knitting and explained that there were nineteen members of the Piper City Friends' Meeting, including herself and her brother Walter, and on Sunday mornings they gathered together at the Franklin Street Meeting House where they sat on two rows of benches arranged around a small central table.

'What about the preacher?'

'No preacher,' said Patience. Instead, they abided in silence and sought the light of God within themselves and no one spoke out loud unless the spirit moved them.

'What light of God?' said Galen Pike.

'The light of God that shines in every man,' said Patience.

On the following day Byron Lym summoned Patience Haig and the pastor of the Episcopalian church and a handful of the other Piper City residents who supported the creation of the hostel for unwed mothers and told them they couldn't have it.

Afterwards, walking home, Patience passed Mayor Lym's big yellow house with its screened-in porch and its magical square of mown green lawn and its herbaceous borders and its sweeping driveway of twinkling smooth-rolled macadam out in front. She passed the schoolhouse with its perished square of flapping tarpaulin tethered to the beams of the broken roof; she passed the plot of unused ground next to the lumber yard where they'd hoped to build the library; the empty warehouse that could so easily be converted into a fever hospital; and by the time she reached Franklin Street she felt so low, so crushed and despondent and depressed, that she didn't go to the jail at all that day to visit Galen Pike.

She ate lunch with her brother Walter and let loose a tirade against the mayor. 'Byron Lym has no interest in the unfortunate people of this world,' she said, speaking quickly and breathlessly. Boiling fury and exasperated irritation bordering on despair made her burst out: 'He is selfish and corrupt and bad for the town.'

Walter served the macaroni cheese and Patience sat without eating, fuming.

Byron Lym had won every election in Piper City for fifteen years. The margin was narrow, but on election day, the Republican vote always seemed to win out: there were enough people in Piper City who didn't seem to mind Byron Lym stealing their taxes and spending them on himself, as long as he kept them low.

'It's wrong, Walter,' she declared, 'the way that man manages to hold onto those votes. It's like a greedy child with a handful of sticky candies and it shouldn't be allowed when there's not one ounce of goodness in him, not one single solitary drop.'

Walter raised his eyebrows and looked at his sister with his mild smile. 'No light of God, sister?'

Patience threw her napkin at him across the table. 'Don't tease me Walter. Doubtless it is there in some dark silk-lined pocket of his embroidered waistcoat but if it is he keeps it well hidden.'

When they'd finished eating she asked her brother to please excuse her, she was going out for some air and for an hour Walter could hear her out on the porch glider, rocking furiously back and forth, the rusty rings creaking and tugging in the porch roof as if they might pull the whole thing down at any moment.

In his cell, Pike sat with the rope cutting into his wrists, the chain grinding against his hips every time he shifted himself in the chair. He looked around at the bare brick walls and the thick bars, at Knapp reading his newspaper or hunched over his skillet or dragging the twigs of his old broom across the office floor.

He closed his eyes and sat listening to the rustle of the aspen trees outside, and from time to time he turned his head and looked out through the tiny window at the maroon peaks of the mountains.

Eleven o'clock had come and gone, then twelve and the woman in the grey dress with the lopsided nose had not appeared. Three o'clock, four, still no sign, and Galen Pike discovered that he missed her.

He missed the gentle tapping of her knitting needles, the soft reedy tooting of the stale air of his cell as it went in and out of her squashed nostril. He realised that from the moment he woke up in the mornings, he was listening for her quick light step in the street outside. From the moment Knapp pushed his oatmeal through the bars and reached in for his potty, he was looking over at the office door and waiting for it to open. She was the only person in the world who did not recoil from him in disgust. In the courthouse people had held themselves against the wall, gawping at his dirty black hair and straggly vagabond's beard, shaking their heads as if they had seen the devil. This one, with her neat hair and her long plain face and her flat polished shoes, sat there straight and stiff and looked him in the eye. He felt bad about calling her an old lady and being rude about her nose. He missed the way she gathered the silence of his cell about her like something warm that did not exclude him from it. He'd even come to enjoy the strawberry cordial.

Slowly, inch by careful inch, and with the greatest difficulty, he began working his hands loose from the tight coils of the rope.

'Forgive me, Mr. Pike,' said Patience when she came in the morning.

She would have come yesterday, she said, but the mayor had turned down their application for the hostel. He said it would be 'a blister in the eye of any visitor to Piper City and an affront to the respectability of its inhabitants'. Afterwards her spirits had been so low she'd gone straight home. 'My company would have been very poor I'm afraid, Mr. Pike, even for someone who makes as few demands on it as you.'

Pike wished Knapp wasn't there. He hated the way the fat jailer spied on them. 'Ain't that a shame,' he said, his voice low, hoarse.

'Yes.'

Suddenly there were tears in Patience Haig's eyes. Her plain narrow face looked even longer than ever, pulled down by the twitching corners of her thin mouth.

Pike studied her. He didn't know what to say.

Knapp had edged closer, attracted no doubt by the soft sound of Patience Haig crying. When Pike saw him he jumped up with his chair on his back and shook his chains and roared and rushed towards the bars like a gorilla, sending the terrified Knapp scurrying back to his stove on the far side of his little office. When Pike returned to the table he found Patience laughing quietly.

'He's like the winged lion in the Book of Revelation,' she said, blowing her nose. 'Full of eyes before, behind and within.'

'Ain't that the truth.'

Patience sniffed and dried her cheeks with a half-made bootie. She straightened her long dry braid and squared her bony shoulders.

'Well,' she said. 'Enough of my disappointments, Mr. Pike. How are you today?'

Pike wanted to tell her he'd missed her yesterday when she hadn't come.

'I'm okay,' he said.

'That's good,' said Patience.

'I have something for you,' said Galen Pike, laying his hand upon the table. He had made it, he said, to brighten her frock.

It was a kind of rosette, or flower, woven from what appeared to be loose threads from the rope that had been twined about his hands, which Patience saw now was no longer there. Four rough stringy petals; at the centre a button from his putrid blood-soaked shirt. Patience held it for a moment in the palm of her hand. The rough petals

117

scraped her skin. She wondered if Pike meant it as a romantic gesture of some sort.

If the preparation of the heart is taken seriously the right words will come.

'Thank you, Mr. Pike,' she said gently. Thank you but she couldn't accept it, she was against adornment, material decoration.

She placed the flower back in the hollow of his cupped hand. His dirty fingers closed around it.

'You hate me.'

'No.'

Knapp held his breath. He watched Pike turn the rope flower over in his hand and shake his head, the foul matted tangle of snakes and rat-tails, and heard him tell Patience Haig she was wrong about the light of God being in every man. He didn't have it. It had passed him by. Where he was, was dark and swampy and bad.

'Nonsense,' said Patience.

It was true, said Pike, looking out through the tiny window at the maroon-coloured peaks beyond. Since his mother died he'd done all manner of wicked things. Since she passed away, years and years and years ago, there'd been no one to tell him how to behave; no one in the world he'd wanted to please, whose good opinion mattered at all. If he'd wanted to do something, he'd gone ahead and done it. He looked at Patience. What was her name? he asked.

'Patience,' she said. 'Patience Haig.'

'You remind me, a little, Miss Haig, of my mother.'

Knapp's beady eyes moved from Galen Pike to the thin Quaker lady in her drab frock. It was hard to tell from her expression if she enjoyed this comparison with Pike's mother. Her face showed no emotion, her long braid lay neatly down her back, her hands folded in her lap.

'I am afraid of the hangman, Miss Haig,' said Galen Pike.

He touched his hand to his throat. Would she shave him, in the morning? And cut his hair? Would she bring him a clean shirt so he wouldn't look so dirty and over-grown when they came for him in the morning? That is, he added with an awkward kind of grimace, if she didn't disapprove too much of him being anxious about his appearance.

Patience looked at her hands. Of course she would shave him, she said softly. If he thought it would help.

And then, because she wanted very much to lighten the heaviness of the moment, she smiled, and said she hoped she wouldn't make too much of a mess of it; she'd watched her brother Walter shaving a few times but had no experience herself. Pike said he was sure it would be all right. He trusted her not to hurt him.

When she'd finished shaving him the next morning, and given him Walter's clean shirt to put on instead of his stinking one, Patience asked him if he wanted her to read something. The twenty-third Psalm was beautiful, she said. It would give him strength, she was sure. Pike said all he wanted was for her to go with him. For ten min-utes more they sat quietly. There was the sound of Knapp's broom moving across the floor of his little office, outside in the yard the rustle of the aspen trees, and then Knapp came with the key, and Sheriff Nye and two of his men, and Dr. Harriman and the hangman from Boulder.

Nye unlocked the chain around Pike's waist and untied the remaining rope that fastened his legs to the chair, and took him by the arm.

In the yard he asked him if he had any last words and in a strong voice Pike said he wanted to thank Miss Patience Haig for the tasty biscuits and the cordial and the clean shirt and the shave but most of all he wanted to thank her for her sweet quiet company. She was the best and kindest person he had ever known. He had not deserved her but he was grateful and he wished he had something to give her, some small remembrance or lasting token of appreciation to show his gratitude, but he had nothing and all he could hope was that if she ever thought of him after he was dead, it would not be badly.

It was hard to tell, Knapp said later to his wife, what effect this short speech of Pike's had on Patience Haig, but when the burlap bag came smartly down over Pike's black eyes and repulsive ravenous features and the floor opened beneath his feet, he was certain Miss Haig struggled with her famous composure; that behind the rough snap of the cloth and the clatter of the scaffold's wooden machinery, he heard a small high cry escape from her plain upright figure.

When it was over Patience asked Knapp if she might sit for a while in the empty cell. She looked for the rope flower but it wasn't there. Knapp must have spirited it away, or perhaps Pike had taken it with him.

It seemed an eternity since he'd first wandered into town. There'd still been snow on the ground, though the worst of the winter had been over. For months before there'd been talk of a little gold to the south, and she remembered seeing the four Piper City men heading off on their expedition to look for it, Pike making the fifth as bag-carrier and general dogsbody, loaded up with cooking pots and shovels, dynamite, fuel, picks.

She walked slowly away from the jailhouse, trying to empty her mind of everything that had happened since the four Piper City men had failed to return and their horrible fate had been discovered. She tried to empty her mind of the quiet hours she'd spent with Galen Pike at the jail, of Byron Lym's crushing rejection of her latest project, of the terrible hanging. She had never felt so miserable in her entire life. She turned out of North Street into Franklin, past the shuttered front of the general store, the closed bank, the locked-up haberdasher's, the drawn blinds of the dentist. She paused before the heavy pine doors of the bank. On the brass knocker someone had tied an evergreen wreath with a thick black ribbon. *Poor Mr. Shrigley*, she thought. *Poor Mr. Palgrave. Poor Damon Archer and Dawson Mew.*

She walked on a little way and then she stopped and turned and looked back at the silent premises of the four dead men.

It had not occurred to her before.

'Oh dear Lord,' she whispered, thinking of Byron Lym's stubborn but wafer-thin majority at the polls.

In Piper City everyone knew how everyone else voted and if Patience's memory served her and she was not mistaken, there'd been forty-eight Republican voters at the last election, and since then Galen Pike had eaten four of them. It was doubtful Lym could succeed next time without them.

Patience turned on her heel.

She squared her bony shoulders and tucked her basket into the crook of her arm.

Quickened her step along Franklin Street towards home.

Ran up the steps onto the porch and in through the screen door, to tell Walter the news.

WICKED FAIRY

Lenny looked sideways at the girl and pictured her rising early that morning, at first light, padding into the cold kitchen of some sort of hostel, and lining everything up on a narrow cluttered counter. She pictured her working the butter quickly into the flour with the chewed ends of her fingers, adding a little iced water and pressing it into a ball and setting it to rest in a large and grubby communal fridge while she got on with separating the eggs and whisking the yolks with the sugar and warming the cream in a pan on the stove.

How thin and sinewy her arms were! And how cold she looked—as if, while the pie crust was baking beneath a layer of tinfoil and kidney beans, she'd gone off to take a shower in some horrible plastic-curtained little cubicle and had never properly warmed up afterwards.

She seemed to Lenny to have appeared from nowhere— to have risen up from the shadows behind the pillar at the end of the crowded pew. A dark-haired, frail-looking thing dressed entirely in black, as if in mourning—a black short-sleeved dress with a worn turtleneck collar, black stockings with snags in them, an old black broad-brimmed hat that was too big and came down almost to her chin.

If Lenny ducked slightly she could see the girl's small sharp-featured face beneath the floppy brim of the big borrowed-looking hat. Fierce pixie eyes and hollow cheeks, a brittle mouth. Everything about her made Lenny think of a string pulled tight and about to be plucked, a figure balanced on the crumbling lip of a cliff and ready to jump; a brief electric calm before a storm.

Who was she?

One of Don's ex-girlfriends? A stalker, a prostitute? A disgruntled employee from his office? A mental patient?

Lenny looked at the pie, in its ancient springform pan, resting on the open palm of the girl's small right hand. It had a blackened fluted crust and it was piled high with a custardy filling. Lenny could smell the vanilla, the fat in the cream. She watched as the girl, like a diminutive baseball pitcher, drew back her thin sinewy arm. Lenny held her breath. She waited for some kind of instinct to kick in but nothing happened, nothing happened that made her cry out in a loud and urgent way LOOK OUT DON!!!! THERE'S A GIRL HERE WITH A PIE!!!! Nothing at all that made her want to run out into the aisle and throw herself like a stampeding elephant across the chancel steps in front of her thirty-five-year-old son and save him from the pie. The only feeling Lenny had as he came striding towards them along the crimson carpet with his flaxen-haired bride on his arm, was that she didn't have any interest in him, or his bride, or the little girls they had with them who were dressed like tiny princesses, or the little boys who were wearing velvet knickerbockers as if they all still lived in the eighteenth century. The only feeling Lenny had as she watched the long slow parabola of the pie moving out into the aisle and travelling like a spinning planet towards his face, was that she preferred this dark-haired girl to any of them; the only feeling she had when the soft squashy sound came, and the muffled cream-filled shout, was that she wanted to reach for the girl's hand and run for the back of the church, fly out through the big doors into the wide and busy street and hail a cab; the only feeling she had when the driver turned and looked at the two of them thrown together in the back—Lenny breathless, her heart racing, the girl still holding onto her hand—was that she'd lived her whole life till now in a kind of dull enchantment, and when the driver asked them, *Where to, ladies?* the only feeling she had was that she was completely, fully awake.

CREED

SHE COULD SEE Creed's place now, up ahead, not more than another three quarters of a mile.

On the big flat stone at the top of the path she stopped to rest, pushed back her sticky hair and wondered again what he would do when he saw her—what he would say and how he would be and what he would look like too, close-up, after all this time.

For years now, for most of her life, she'd seen him only from afar, mending his walls or checking on his sheep or coming down off the high fell with a bucket to the spring above the waterfall, a bulky hatted figure.

A few times over the years she'd thought about going up there and knocking on his door and saying to him, *Michael it's me. Ruth. From the valley. Come. Sit with me at least.*

Once not long after her thirtieth birthday she'd come up this far along the path with a box of her brother's old dominoes in her pocket. All the way along the river and up over the slick black rocks on the west side of the beck to the top, with the game's smooth pieces chinking against each other and her thumb fidgeting with the sliding wooden lid, she'd rehearsed what she'd say to Creed when she reached him: that it was crazy, idiotic, them living like this—the two of them in this vast forgotten garden of bracken and stone and pasture and bog, like the very last people on earth, but never speaking, never coming close to one another.

She'd pictured them both at his table, her brother's dominoes spread out between them in various arrangements, not speaking perhaps (neither of them had much practice at that) but at least sitting together in a not-uncomfortable silence. Then up here at the big flat stone at the top of the path she'd lost her nerve. In the distance, his thick-walled bothy with its arrow-slit windows had looked so closed-in and stubborn and hunched against the weather and the world, so like a fortress for his feelings, that she'd lacked the courage to go on and had turned around and gone back down.

Today she was wearing her brown work boots and her black coat and her blue dress and she hoped she looked respectable. She didn't want Michael Creed to open his door and look at her and think she was a fright.

She'd been a child when his wife died, ten or eleven years old.

She remembered the two of them coming to her father's church. The wife's dark hair. Creed a young man, broad-shouldered and strong, with a neat beard.

Her father had gone up there a dozen times afterwards and tried to comfort him but Creed wouldn't let him in the house. She remembered how tired and discouraged her father had looked the last time he came home.

'What happened, William? What did he say to you?' her mother had asked, rather fearfully, and they'd all watched him hang up his coat and press his lips together and set down his Bible on their kitchen table and tap it lightly with his fingers. He'd looked as if he was debating with himself whether to repeat in front of his family what Creed had said.

'He said, Janice, that God had greatly disappointed him. He said that he had begged Him for His pity and His mercy and had been refused. He said there was nothing now I had to tell him that he wanted to listen to and if I ever came trespassing on his land again and tried to talk to him about God's love, he would come out into his yard and stick his shotgun in my crap-filled mouth and shoot me.'

Creed stayed away from the church after that, and if he ever came face to face with her father down in the valley he turned around and walked the other way. He began to avoid anyone who attended the Sunday service, which in those days had been nearly everyone. At some point he moved out of the farmhouse he'd shared with his wife and into the bothy further up the fell. Eventually he stopped coming down into the valley for anything. It was as if, not being able to look God in the eye and spit in His face, or inform Him personally that he was sending Him to Coventry forever, Creed had settled on the next best thing. Or perhaps he'd decided that there was no face to spit in and he was living in a world of fools; that from now on, he was on his own.

He mended his walls and birthed his ewes and when autumn came he drove the new season's lambs up along the high straight track that had once been the Romans' way north to the border, sold them to be slaughtered, picked up his supplies and walked back the way he'd come. Anywhere he had to go, he took the old Roman way, never the path down into the valley, the track along the river that took him past their house and the church.

What would he look like?

Like the other men she remembered in their fifties and sixties who used to live here? Bull-necked men with brick-red faces and bow legs and giant hands?

When he was young his hair had been brown, chest-nut-coloured, she remembered that.

Not as dark as his wife's but still brown. His beard had been brown also.

And hadn't he had one brown eye and one grey? She thought so. She thought she remembered her sister Pam remarking on it once when they were girls.

Her sister Pam and her brother Frank always asked after him when they came. 'And what about Michael Creed?' they said. 'Do you ever see him, Ruth? Is he still up there?'

'Yes,' she told them. 'He's still up there.'

But what if he wasn't?

What if since the last time she'd glimpsed his bulky shape in the distance, he'd died or given up at last and gone away, like everyone else?

What if she got there and knocked on his door and there was no answer and when she pushed it open the place was empty and cleared out and there was nothing up there but his sheep and a couple of starving dogs?

In winter, months went by sometimes without a sign of him. Then there'd be a storm, a heavy fall of snow, and he'd be up there with his dogs, digging out his buried sheep. The dogs trickling over the white hillside, showing him where to put his shovel so he could bring them out alive. In spring, around lambing time, she woke sometimes in the dark and saw the pinprick beam of his flashlight moving over the sloping fields as he went about checking on things.

Over the years her father's scattered parish had dwindled away.

One by one the farms had emptied out. The old had died, the young and the middle-aged had moved away. Where there'd been two shops and a pub, a school and a recreation room there were only the carcasses of buildings. When her father died, no one was sent to replace him. Where there'd been people and families and children there was only her left now, and Michael Creed.

Who would have thought a place could fall in on itself so quickly? That so monumental a ruin could be achieved like that? Almost, it seemed to her sometimes, it had happened in the blink of an eye, or in the course of one brief night while she slept.

Hikers who came up this far poked their faces in at her window. They seemed amazed to see curtains, chimney smoke, her boots at the door. Once, coming back from the church, she'd found a young couple in woollen hats and waterproof jackets on the step at the back of her house, picnicking on crisps and sandwiches and hot tea from a thermos. They'd hardly seemed to believe her when she said she lived here, and when they'd gone she thought of them telling their friends about the woman they'd found living way up at the far end of the valley by herself, using the words she'd overheard her sister Pam and her brother Frank whispering to each other when they came and thought she was outside, words like squalid, primitive, unhygienic.

For a time, she'd let her brother and sister drive her back with them for a few days. But in town she discovered, as the years went by, that her clothing attracted attention, that her appearance shocked people. One cold Christmas when Pam came to collect her she'd got in the car wearing both her dresses, her blue one and her knitted fawn one, one on top of the other. Pam had been ashamed. All that week Ruth saw her making silent signals with her eyes to her friends. She discovered also that she'd aged more quickly than these people. Carting water off the fell to her house in a bucket, hauling fodder from the pasture on a sledge for her cow Charlotte, chopping wood and break-ing sticks and stuffing them into the stove and picking up scraps of slate off the hills to mend her roof—it had all made her age more rapidly than Pam and these other women who came to Pam's house and tried not to gawp when Pam said, 'This is my younger sister, Ruth.' Like Pam, all the women still had dark hair and neat unbroken fingernails and attractive teeth. She couldn't imagine how they managed it. She cared a little about it, this difference between the way they looked and the way she did, but not much. She told Pam she'd not be going back with her again. She was happy where she was, she'd no urge now to leave.

She'd stayed on to look after the church. When no one came to replace her father, it had been impossible for her to think of leaving it untended and unused. In winter she put holly in the alcoves. In spring, hawthorn and valerian. On Sundays she stood in the cold in front of the empty pews and read aloud the lesson. She patched the roof and polished the coloured window in the nave and the blackened script engraved on the brass plaque her father had screwed into the lintel over the door when he first arrived here from the coast. It was still her favourite Psalm: *I will lift up mine eyes unto the hills from whence cometh my help. My help cometh from the Lord.*

In the back behind her house she grew swede and onions and potatoes and spinach. She had apples and blackcurrants and gooseberries from the trees and bushes her mother had planted. In winter an arsenal of things preserved in jars. A taxi came nine miles up the valley track once every three months and drove her to Penrith for her shopping. Her sister and her brother visited twice a year from Carlisle. She had no phone and no television but she had chickens and her cow and a sewing machine and her father's books. She knew that there was another kind of world and she could see that it had its attractions but she did not want to live in it. She wanted to be here.

She liked it here. She was forty-two and she had not been lonely, not really. She had never lived her life expecting it to change.

Around her neck she wore the small wooden cross that had belonged to her father and as she walked she touched it every now and again to make sure it was still hidden beneath her dress.

She'd tried to leave it behind but in the end she'd not been able to.

She'd unhooked the clasp and dropped the chain into the palm of her hand and tipped it onto a plate and stepped out of the door but when she got to the path she'd felt so naked and afraid without it that she'd gone back and put it back on and slipped it inside her dress, telling herself that Creed wouldn't necessarily see it. However things went, she would do everything she could to hide it from him.

As she walked her legs shook.

Her damp face boiled with heat, her blue dress clung to her like another skin, her heart thumped like a big beating wheel. She took off her black coat, folded it over her arm, and carried it. She wished she could turn back here and go back down to the beck and splash her face and cool her throat with the icy water.

Above her, a pair of peregrines rose in circles and vanished high up over the crags, into the blue. From beneath she could see the yellow flashes of their legs, the black streaks of their tails and wingtips and as she watched them she imagined looking down out of the sky at the dark speck of herself moving slowly over the pale brown hills towards Creed's bothy. The ground was boggy here, up on the higher ground after the path gave out. As she plodded through it the stiff grass brushed her bare knees.

She wished she didn't resemble her father. She wished she wasn't tall as he'd been. She wished she didn't have his springy hair and large beaky nose and pointy chin. She didn't want Creed to open his door and think of her father and think that after all these years she'd come to him on some kind of religious mission. She didn't want him to be surly and unwelcoming. She didn't want him to slam the door in her face or bellow at her through one of his narrow windows and tell her to be gone. She didn't want him to pull his gun on her. She wished she'd come up here that other day, with the dominoes. She wished this wasn't her first time. She wished that the ice had been broken between them before now—that she could at least have become an ordinary neighbour to him. *Come on, Michael, it's just us now. Sit with me. Everyone else has gone. The old have died, the young are all in the towns. My brother Frank, remember? My sister Pam? They're in Carlisle. Pam's a nurse. Frank's at one of the big hotels. The Glaisters have all gone. Partingtons too, and Capsticks and Pickthalls and Hawksmiths, all upped and gone.*

She wondered what Creed made of it all, this emptying out. She wondered what he felt when he turned up at the slaughterhouse with his new season's lambs, or went into the places he visited for his supplies. She wondered if the people there exchanged secret glances and if he was made to feel uncomfortable. She wondered if he felt like she did and if in spite of everything that had happened in his life, he was always glad to come home.

There was more wind up here.

It cooled her face and made a rushing sound through the stiff grass and the bracken, a sound her father always used to say was the same sound he'd grown up with, the sound of the sea. When he said that, her sister Pam used to beg him to take them all on holiday somewhere to the coast, to Morecambe or Blackpool, somewhere sandy and warm where they could stretch out on towels and go bathing and eat ice cream and see the lights and a show, and every year that they didn't go she told Ruth that the first bloody chance she got, she was off out of here, away from this boring fucking dump of a valley, these prehistoric hills and struggling miserable little farms.

Up ahead now, only another hundred yards, Creed's bothy sat like a dark stone resting in the bottom of a deep smooth-sided bowl. All around it the tawny ramparts of the hills rose to the sky. There'd been no question this morning of setting off towards anything else; there'd been no question of the nine mile walk along the river to a road where she might sit for an hour and wait without a single vehicle passing. With each step now she felt her own slow, dragging gravity. Across the marshy ground she proceeded with difficulty and sometimes she stumbled.

His yard was bordered by a woodshed and a privy and the L-shaped dwelling part of the bothy itself. Turf and ferns and a spongy blanket of moss grew on the thick shaley roof slates. The bothy door was painted brown. Bronze lichen grew on his walls like rust. A trio of his black-faced sheep burst out from behind them when they saw her coming, bunching together and jostling each other in their hurry to get away, as if she was something dangerous.

Oh Jesus, what would he say to her? Would he be appalled by the sight of her? Would he know who she was? Would he hold that against her? Would he look past her through the open brown door and out beyond the opening in his yard across the soggy uplands and the pale brown hills and down into the long tapering valley with its scattered emptied farms and ask her how in glory's name it had happened? Would he turn sarcastic and ask her if she'd had a visit from the Holy Spirit?

At the corner of his yard a rowan tree grew out of the stones. She leaned against it, breathed. The hour's walk, the climb, had taken her half the day. Her hair felt prickly and dry as gorse. There was bog cotton in it, grass and cuckoo spit. Blood leaked out of her, filling her boots and coating the ground. She'd known since this morning that something was wrong.

She could no longer recall the Scotsman's face, only his sandy hair and his pale body.

When he was gone she realized she didn't know his name or the name of his town or what job he did in the rest of his life or if he had a wife and children. She wasn't used to conversation and they'd hardly talked.

He told her he'd come over Rampsgill Head and round Blea Tarn and after that the fog had come down and he'd had no compass and had to continue on his hands and knees, worried that he'd turned himself round and wasn't where he thought he was and that on one side or the other there might be nothing but crag and scree and a sheer plunging drop to the bottom. When he saw her light he'd thought at first it must be the sun or the moon, a small whitish glow in the murk.

In the morning he'd thanked her for the hot break-fast and her warm bed. He was glad the ugly weather had brought him to her door, he said. He'd had a nice time.

She could see nothing now, even in the daylight every-thing was dark and all she could feel was the raised lump of the cross at her throat. She wished she hadn't worn it. She was afraid again it might make Creed angry, that any-thing like that might disgust him still, that he'd send her away. She began to tug at the chain and fumble with the clasp at the back of her neck. Her last mad thought was that she wished there was some way she could tidy herself up. At least put a comb through her hair.

Creed's dogs found her in his yard.

He didn't recognise her but he knew she must be one of the Reverend's daughters from the valley, whichever one had stayed behind. He could see the bevelled edges of a crucifix beneath the blue fabric of her dress. He couldn't remember her name but over the years he'd seen her many times, a dark point down there, moving between her house and the church. He'd seen the cars that once in a while fetched her away then brought her back along the track beside the river. Her lips moved a little and he wondered if she was praying. There was blood on the stony earth of his yard. A large clot, dark and ragged like liver on the hem of her dropped black coat.

Creed was brawny and white-haired and tall. He lifted her up and carried her inside and put her on his bed. In his whole life he had never seen so much blood.

At the sink he rolled up his sleeves and scrubbed himself and slipped his right arm up inside her. He moved his hand up past the torn and pulsing placenta and found the breeched legs, the curving beads of the small spine. Ruth's eyelids fluttered and Creed didn't tell her that she'd come too late. He knelt by the bed and stroked her hair and told her in a soft voice that she was a good girl, a brave girl. He repeated the same whispered words over and over the way he did with his sheep when they couldn't birth and they were suffering and miserable; and when he was sure there was no more time and no other way he boiled up a pan and went in under the breastbone with his razor and brought out the child, a tiny curled-up girl with a pointy chin and a small beaky nose and a glistening cap of sand-coloured hair, and when the long night ended and morning came and Creed had done everything he could with his boiled cloths and his needle and his fine cotton thread, when he'd tried every desperate thing short of a prayer to stop the blood and there was nothing at all, now, that could be done and it was over, he went and stood for a long time looking out through one of his arrow-slit windows at the sloping fell aflame in the dawn with the child in his arms.

She was light as a leaf and just as beautiful.

He'd call her Rowan, after the tree in his wall.

He wished his wife could see her.

NOTHING LIKE MY NIGHTMARE

THE DAY SHE left I thought of all the things that could go wrong: that she'd lose her passport or her glasses or run out of anti-bacterial handwash. Or the nuns wouldn't be there to meet her and take her to the school as they'd promised. Or she'd go to the cash machine her first day in the city and it wouldn't give her any money. Or she'd get a blister on her foot like the one she got in Solva last summer from her new sandal and it would get infected and she wouldn't go to the doctor in time and it would grow gangrenous and she'd end up having to have her leg amputated, or she'd have brought the wrong kind of adapter, or the travel towel she'd bought from Millets would be worse than useless, or her plane would crash, exploding in a ball of black fire somewhere high above the mountains—but when we got there, the old man in the bright shawl said it was nothing like that. It just broke in two like a bread roll, spilling crumbs from the sky.

SIBYL

Sibyl (si · bil) **1.** One of various women of antiquity who were reputed to possess powers of prophecy or divination.

—*The Shorter Oxford English Dictionary*

FOR A WHILE now, Sibyl Hadley has been watching the umbrella boy from her rented deck chair.

He is wearing a pair of long turquoise shorts patterned all over with big white flowers and tied loosely in front, with laces, like a pair of shoes. He has beads in his hair and a smooth golden chest and smooth arms with ropy veins visible beneath the skin, a rise and then a hollow around each low-lying hip bone above the dangling laces of his flower-splashed shorts.

He doesn't seem to feel the cold—he isn't, as far as she can tell, shivering even slightly in the wind, in the bright chilly sunshine. Sibyl herself is wrapped up like a parcel in layers of warm clothing—trousers and tights and a polo-neck sweater, a quilted waterproof jacket with the hood up. She has taken off her reading glasses and laid her book facedown across her lap in order to watch the boy as he goes about his work, planting the long metal spikes of the umbrellas in the damp sand, making sure they are securely buried and canted into the wind, then carefully unfurling their fluttering canvas shades.

He'd smiled at her when she'd gone to the door of his little wooden hut to pay for her deck chair, and when she'd given him the money for it and her thumb had brushed against the skin of his open palm, it had sent a rush of feeling through the whole of her body.

He's busy now, locked in a struggle with the rising wind, trying to shake out the heavy folded shade on the last of the umbrellas, all of which, like the deck chairs, are available for rent, either by the day or by the hour. There. He's done it. Sibyl watches him brushing the wet sand from his hands onto his shorts and shaking his beaded hair like a dog drying itself.

There are tears in Sibyl's eyes when she looks away, out across the flat grey water of the Channel and over at the peeling ochre façade of the old casino at the far end of the beach near the town.

'Dear God,' she whispers into the wind. 'How did I get so old?'

From the dining room of the Hôtel Mercure, Wade Abello looks out across the boardwalk to where the Englishwoman is sitting, bundled up in her deck chair with her book on her lap, looking out across the sea.

At the market in town this morning he has bought her a dusty rough-hewn bar of handmade lavender soap. It is wrapped in a brown paper bag and he is holding it now in his enormous right hand.

He is a vast, pear-shaped man, Wade Abello, the owner of a feed store in Mason, Wyoming, and clad, today, in a huge pair of khaki trousers with an elasticized waistband, a neatly pressed short-sleeved shirt of peppermint green cotton seersucker that might otherwise do duty as a slipcover for a good-sized armchair.

He knows her name is Sibyl Hadley because he has read it upside down in the maroon leather register at the front desk in the lobby.

'Sibyl,' he practises, feeling his heartbeat quicken.

Yesterday, at the church in Dives, he'd looked in through the leper's hole and seen her at the altar, praying.

She didn't kneel but her head was bowed and her eyes were closed and her hands were clasped together under her chin.

He'd stood there for a long time, holding his breath and wondering what it was that a woman like Sibyl Hadley might be praying for at her age; if, by any chance, it might possibly be the same thing that he is.

When the time had come for the minibus to leave the church and bring them back to the hotel, he'd considered asking her if he could sit next to her, but she was at the front and in the end he hadn't been confident that he could fit into the narrow seat at her side without most of his body hanging out over the aisle, which would have meant that he'd have been blocking it when the young German family and the Italian new-lyweds boarded the bus and wanted to get by. So he'd moved past her and sat down near the back and looked at the top of her head and now and then, when the sun went behind a cloud and the windows went dark, at the reflection of her face in the glass as they drove back along the coast.

It's been a disappointment to Sibyl that even though it is not yet the end of August, the Hôtel Mercure is less than half-full.

Aside from herself, the only guests are a young German family and an Italian couple on their honeymoon, a fat American man in a luminous green shirt who looks at his feet whenever she smiles at him and has yet to address a single word in her direction.

It's the weather, apparently, that's keeping people away—the cold and the unseasonable wind. The days are quiet and the nights are empty, the only sounds things she wishes she didn't have to hear: the noisy whooping of the wind outside her window, and the even noisier whooping of the Italian newlyweds in the room next to hers.

Three times now they have woken her in the small hours; she can hear them through the wall. Three nights running they have woken her and she has lain there till dawn beneath the crisp clean sheets of her comfortable double bed unable to go back to sleep.

Yesterday at the church in Dives she'd prayed.

After listening to the guide tell them about the bless-ing of the Norman ships before they set off on their conquering journey across the Channel, she'd walked up to the altar and bowed her head and clasped her hands together and prayed and then immediately felt ridiculous.

It was years since she'd set foot in a church except to look at the things inside, and even if she still said things like 'Heaven help me' and 'God forbid' she no longer believed they had any power or meaning.

Perhaps that had been part of the problem, believing that they did. Perhaps her mistake had been to tell herself, as the years slipped by, that what happened or didn't happen in this life was of no importance; that none of it really mattered because if you were patient and did not dwell on things too much, your reward would come later. Well she didn't think that any more, especially since her illness. Her prayer yesterday had been, in every possible way, a nonsense, an aberration, and all the way back to the hotel on the minibus she'd scolded herself for doing something so stupid and pathetic. For an hour and a half after they got back to town she'd walked along the beach, all the way up to the Roches Noires and back, gulping down the air.

Looking now at the umbrella boy, it occurs to her that she could pay him.

There's a piece of orange nylon rope knotted around the handle of the open door to his little wooden hut and it looks to her as if the door could be tied shut.

It would be dark inside which she thinks on balance she'd probably prefer. Even though she would like to see him she is shy about him seeing her.

She closes her hand around the folded notes in the pocket of her quilted jacket and counts them with her fingers; wonders if what she has with her is likely to be enough, or if he might ask for more.

There are other things in her life she always thought would happen that never did, but this is the only one of them, she's discovered lately, that seems important. It is the only one of them, now, she really, really minds about.

In her head, in her best French, she rehearses a form of words that will convey to the boy what it is she wants; what it is she has somehow ended up going her entire life without.

What Wade pictures is him and the Englishwoman hiking up to one of the flat alpine meadows in the mountains above his brown-shingled house in Mason.

The two of them tucking into a picnic of cold grilled chicken sandwiches with mustard mayonnaise on thick slices of fresh rye bread. Some cold beers. A few slices of apricot Danish from the bakery over in Marbleton. Maybe some crumbly Canadian cheddar and a box of handmade chocolates.

Then both of them shedding all their clothes—his khaki pants and his peppermint shirt, her padded trousers and her sweater and her quilted waterproof jacket—the two of them together out in the open air in Wyoming on top of a mattress of tough flattened grass with the remains of their picnic around them; he, Wade Abello, doing everything perfectly—knowing, somehow, exactly what to do; the Englishwoman called Sibyl Hadley throwing back her head and yodelling with pleasure and delight and a low deep-throated shudder of relief.

With her hand curled around the money in her pocket Sibyl runs through in her head the words of her short but, she hopes, clear speech.

She goes over it several times, making various changes and corrections, hesitating over whether to use 'je veux' or 'je voudrais', *I want* or *I would like*, and then she stops.

The boy is in his hut now, leaning against the frame of the open door. He has finished putting up his umbrellas and is smoking a cigarette.

Sibyl looks at him, watches the gentle rise and fall of his chest, the movement of his lips, and slowly her fingers uncurl from around the money in the pocket of her coat. The folded notes slip free of her empty hand, and for the second time today her eyes fill with tears. She knows that it is beyond her to ask him, that she cannot possibly do it, and it comes to her then, to Sibyl, in almost the same moment and with all the clarity of a vision or a prophecy, as she sits alone in her rented deck chair on the beach in Trouville in the last week of an unseasonably cold August in the summer of her sixty-seventh year, that the only event now of any importance she can reasonably expect to experience in what remains of her life is likely to be her own death.

It's a terrible thought—it's a terrible thought and it is, you may remember, a windy day.

It's a *very* windy day in fact, and even though the gold-en-skinned umbrella boy has worked hard to make sure that each one of his big stripy parasols is properly canted into the wind—its heavy cotton-fringed shade angled low to the ground, its sharp metal spike dug deep down into the sand and securely buried—you'll understand how easy it is for an especially violent gust to snatch one of the umbrellas up and send it cartwheeling along the beach like a tomahawk or an accessory in a knife-throwing act or something thrown by a gladiator across the dusty floor of the Coliseum.

You'll understand, also, that there's something about the low-slung design of an old-fashioned deck chair that makes it difficult for someone like Sibyl Hadley, in their mid-to-late sixties, to get out of one in a hurry. You'll understand that she is indeed about to die; that in these last split-seconds the whole of her solitary and unfulfilled life is about to flash before her in a quick grey kaleidoscope of drab and joyless scenes.

And yet you will know, too, in your heart, that some very big, very fat men are also surprisingly fast runners—you will know that when Wade Abello has finished shaking the flaky crumbs from his croissant out of his napkin and onto his plate in the dining room of the Hôtel Mercure and pushed back his chair and walked outside and begun to make his lumbering slow-footed way along the boardwalk carrying what looks like his lunch in a paper bag—you will know that when he sees what's happening he will break at once into a thunderous sprint of astonishing power and velocity and when his enormous right hand finally hurls away the bag with its dusty cake of handmade soap inside and his outstretched fingers reach out and grasp instead the spinning cotton fringe of the murderous parasol and he falls to his knees in front of Sibyl in the sand—you will know, then, that Sibyl was wrong about the future, and that this, is just the beginning.

NOTES & ACKNOWLEDGEMENTS

My thanks to the editors of the publications, anthologies and online magazines where a number of these stories (sometimes in a slightly different form) first appeared: *The Dublin Review*; *Granta New Writing*; *The Hippocrates Prize*; *Love Sunday Magazine*; *New Short Stories 3* and *New Short Stories 4* (both Willesden Herald Prize anthologies); *The Manchester Fiction Prize*; *Prospect*; *Red Room New Short Stories Inspired by the Brontës*; *The Royal Society of Literature Review*; *Salamander*; *The Ship*; *The Stinging Fly*; *The Story: Love, Loss and the Lives of Women: 100 Great Short Stories*. Special thanks to Brendan Barrington and Declan Meade, to my agent Rachel Calder, my editor Jen Hamilton-Emery, to Chris Hamilton-Emery and to New Writing North for the financial assistance of a 2013 Northern Writers' Award, supported by Arts Council England.

NOTE ON 'BONNET'

Brontë biographers and scholars have long speculated on what the true nature of the relationship between Charlotte Brontë and her young publisher, George Smith, might have been. We know that Smith was handsome, charming, and clever and that he became Charlotte's good friend, frequent correspondent and attentive host when she visited London; her letters suggest that she may well also have been in love with him and that he knew it. Against the background of Charlotte's tragic family history, her desperate loneliness and sense of personal inadequacy, it is one of the most poignant stories of unrequited love I've ever come across. In my imagination, the encounter depicted in 'Bonnet' takes place towards the end of 1853, when—and these are the facts—Charlotte is 37 and Smith is 29 and has recently become engaged to Elizabeth Blakeway, the beautiful daughter of a wealthy London wine merchant, but no one, including Smith himself, has told Charlotte yet. The historical truth is that Smith seems to have felt unable to break the news to Charlotte, prevaricating and writing to tell her, eventually, only after she has found it out from his mother. When she does, at last, receive his letter, Charlotte writes back what must be, as Brontë scholar Juliet Barker says, 'the most extraordinary letter of congratulation ever written'*:

> *My dear Sir*
> *In great happiness, as in great grief—words of sympathy should be few. Accept my meed of congratulation—and believe me*
> *Sincerely yours*
> *C. Brontë*

Charlotte married the Reverend Arthur Bell Nicholls, curate at Haworth, in June 1854. She died in March 1855 at the age of 38, probably of tuberculosis aggravated by acute morning sickness.

The Brontës : A Life in Letters

ABOUT THE AUTHOR

Carys Davies is the author of two collections of short stories, *The Redemption of Galen Pike* and *Some New Ambush*. She is the winner of the Frank O'Connor International Short Story Award, the Jerwood Fiction Uncovered Prize, the Royal Society of Literature's V.S. Pritchett Memorial Prize, the Society of Authors' Olive Cook Short Story Award, a Northern Writers' Award and a 2016/17 Cullman Fellowship at the New York Public Library. Born in Wales, she now lives in north west England.